Mary Seymour

Tom's Crucifix And Other Tales

Mary Seymour

Tom's Crucifix And Other Tales

ISBN/EAN: 9783337342746

Printed in Europe, USA, Canada, Australia, Japan

Cover: Foto ©Andreas Hilbeck / pixelio.de

More available books at **www.hansebooks.com**

TOM'S CRUCIFIX,

And other Tales.

BY

M. F. S.,

AUTHOR OF "CATHERINE HAMILTON," "THE THREE WISHES,"
"STORIES OF THE SAINTS," "CATHERINE GROWN OLDER,"
"FLUFFY," "LEGENDS OF THE SAINTS," "STORIES
OF MARTYR PRIESTS," ETC., ETC.

Second   Thousand.

London:
R. WASHBOURNE, 18 PATERNOSTER ROW.
1877.

Dedicated

TO THE

BOYS AND GIRLS

OF THE

CONFRATERNITY OF S. CHARLES.

CONTENTS.

PREFACE.

BY AN OBLATE FATHER OF S. CHARLES.

THESE little stories aim at putting Catholic practices in an interesting way before children. Teachers of Christian doctrine to the young, who gather together in our churches on Sunday afternoons, find it difficult to retain the attention of their classes during the whole hour of instruction.

Zeal for their work makes them seek for some means of pleasing those they teach, and perhaps no way is so effective as telling a tale. But to have one ready, which will illustrate the lesson of Catechism, is not the gift of every teacher. The next best thing to a well-told story is a well-written one, and if half one of these is read, there will probably be an eager waiting for its conclusion, .which will give the teacher power over the class. It is hoped, however, that these tales will do more than interest—they are intended to implant a love for those practices of the faith which distinguish the every-day life of a real Catholic from the unbelieving.

FEAST OF S. CHARLES,
November, 1873.

TOM'S CRUCIFIX.

T was a bitterly cold winter night; the snow which had been falling all day had ceased now, but the wind was keen, and little Tom Rogers shivered in his ragged clothing as he sank down upon a door-step and tried in vain to warm his hands by blowing upon them. He had been out since early morning with his broom; standing by the crossing, he had swept over the bustling London street with little success, for nearly every one had passed him by or bidden him " earn his living respectably," and so at last Tom had given it up for that day as a bad job, and was sitting down to rest before he turned homewards.

It was a wretched place to call home—the

dirty court, where he lived in a miserable kitchen, with a woman who was sometimes kind and sometimes cross, depending very much upon his earnings. She wasn't his mother. There were two or three more children in the dirty room, who were hers, but she treated them much as she did Tom, turning them into the streets to get on as best they could.

Just opposite to where Tom sat on the door-step there was a cook's shop, and the very sight of the meat and pudding and sausages made him hungrier than ever, and the worst was he dared not spend one of the few pennies he had earned that day—he would be beaten enough as it was.

It was not exactly fear which made Tom so unwilling to go home; he was so used to rough words and blows that he had ceased to care very much about them; he only lingered because there was nothing much to go in for, and it wouldn't be a great deal warmer in the damp fireless kitchen than in the street.

So Tom sat still and buried his face in his hands, and began wishing ever so many things. First he wished he was the lamplighter; he had often watched him going his rounds, thinking it must be capital fun, because he always went along so cheerfully and quickly. Next he thought it would be rather good to drive an omnibus, and race all the other omnibuses and cabs that went along the street. And then he began just to wish he had money enough to buy slices of pudding and sausage-rolls at the cook's shop as often as he felt hungry.

So his thoughts came back to his own misery, and as he glanced across once more to the tempting shop, his eyes filled with tears, and letting his head fall on his knees he cried bitterly because he was so very cold and hungry, and he knew there was no chance of supper for him that night.

Presently he felt a cold nose rubbing against his hands, and looking up, saw a shabby brown dog, which wagged its tail and whined piteously, almost as if it was sorry for him, and which would not be driven away by kicks or threats, such as Tom was used to give stray dogs who followed him.

"Here's Bouncer, mother," said a child's voice. "Bouncer! come, sir!" but the dog would not stir, only wagged its tail again and looked at Tom.

"What's the matter, my lad?" said the child's mother, who came up just then; but Tom said not a word. "Come, you might tell me what you're crying for," she repeated.

"You'd cry yourself, maybe, if you was as hungry as me," the boy muttered sullenly, for he was rather ashamed of his tears, and had not reckoned on any one seeing them there on the doorstep.

"Well, why don't you go home and get your supper, then?"

"I shan't get no supper, I'll only get thrashed; but I don't care, I'll run away one of these times, that I will."

"Run away from your mother and father? Oh no, you won't do that," said the kind voice.

"Ain't got no mother and father; I only lives along with Nancy."

"Is she good to you?" asked the child, who had been listening in silence till then.

"No, she isn't, but I don't care; I shan't go home at all to-night;" and Tom settled himself again on the doorstep, and put his head down upon his hands as if he wasn't going to say another word.

The woman hardly liked to pass on and leave

him, yet she could not help it, so calling the dog off they went away, and after a while Tom fell fast asleep, and didn't wake until he felt some one shaking him and heard the policeman's voice bidding him " move on."

Then he slunk off another way and lay down under an archway, where he slept in peace until the noises in the streets began, and he knew that day had come again.

He ventured to spend a penny from his pocket in a roll at the first baker's shop he saw open, and he stole a can of milk he found outside the area of a house he passed, and then he made off as fast as he could to his crossing to begin once more his old cry, " Please remember the sweeper."

He got on a little better that day, though ; so towards afternoon he ventured to turn home-wards and see what was going on there : but as he reached the court he was greeted by a tribe of dirty urchins of his own kind, who told him " Nancy had gone clean away, and the room was shut up."

Truly enough it was so; and though Tom had never cared for the rough woman who had taken charge of him as long as he could remember anything, his heart sank very low as he understood for the first time what it was to be homeless and quite alone in the world.

It was useless standing looking at the closed room, though; besides, the children were all laughing at his unhappy face, thinking it capital fun; so he turned away again, and went back to look into the window of his favourite shop, and then, taking some coppers from his pocket, he went in and bought several slices of the pudding which had looked so tempting the night before.

He crossed over to the same doorstep where he had cried from cold and hunger, and sitting down, ate his dinner, and began to wonder what he should do next.

Soon after, the very same dog and child and woman passed along whom he had seen the previous night, and they stopped to speak to him.

" Well, did you get some supper, after all ?" asked the woman.

" I didn't go home; I slept out o' doors; I often does."

" But you'll go home to-night, I hope ?"

Tom grinned.   "I ain't got no home to go to; Nancy's hooked it !"

" *Hooked* it !" exclaimed the woman with a

puzzled face, not quite taking in the boy's meaning.

"Yes; when I went home to-day, she'd cut; the whole lot of 'em's gone, and the place is shut. I don't care; I ain't a bit sorry; I'll get on somehow."

"But that is terrible," said the woman; "whatever can you do?"

"Must do as best I can," said the boy with another grin, as if he rather enjoyed the joke.

"Surely you don't *like* to live such a life, running about the streets, looking so wild and dirty. Wouldn't you like to get your living respectably?"

"That's what all the folks tells me," said Tom scornfully; "them as is too mean to give me a copper. What's the use of telling me to ' earn my living respectably?' Why don't somebody show me how?"

The woman was silent for a minute. She felt it was so true what the boy had said, and yet it was so difficult to know *how* to help him.

"Would you like to come home with me to-night?" she said slowly. "I'm only a poor woman myself, and I have to work hard for my living; still I can't bear to leave you like this

I've just lost a boy myself, no bigger than you; you could sleep where he did for a night or two."

Tom made no difficulty in accepting the offer, but rose from the doorstep at once, saying he'd "like it uncommonly."

"Has he run away, or what's come of him?" he asked as they walked along—a strange-looking party; Mrs. Kelly and Mary, cleanly though poorly dressed; Tom, with his broom under his arm, in all his rags and dirt; and Bouncer, who jumped up against first one and then the other, not quite knowing what to make of it.

"*He?* who do you mean?" said Mrs. Kelly.

"Your boy, as you said you'd lost."

"Oh, he's dead: not three months ago, and I miss him sadly. Ah, he was a good lad to me;" and Mrs. Kelly sighed.

Tom said no more, but trudged along in silence until Bouncer stopped at a house where they all went in.

It was only a kitchen: much such an one as Tom had always lived in; only this was as clean as hands could make it, while Nancy's had been as dirty as was well possible. Tom stared all round, and then sat down on the edge of one of the three rickety chairs that were there, feeling awkward and uncomfortable.

Meanwhile Mrs. Kelly and her little girl put three cups and saucers on the table, and lit a fire, and set on a small kettle ; and then a loaf and a basin of dripping were brought out from a cupboard by the fireplace, and Tom was told to draw up his chair and have some tea.

" I ain't so hungry to-night," he said ; " I've had my dinner, and I had some breakfast too."

" Why, how did you manage that ?" asked Mrs. Kelly.

" Oh, I bought my dinner at the cook's shop; I allers do when I've got any coppers ; and I prigged some milk this morning, and that was capital."

" You *stole* it, did you ?" said Mrs. Kelly gravely.

Tom nodded his head: "Yes, I takes anything I finds. Finding's keeping, you know."

" I know it's very wicked, and that God must be angry with you. Don't you know the Commandments ?"

Tom stared at her in utter surprise, but said nothing.

"Don't you know anything about God, then?"

"Dunno," said the boy, looking puzzled.

"Did you never hear that it was wicked to take other people's things—that God has said, 'Thou shalt not steal'?"

But the boy seemed highly amused. "I knows people gets sent to jail sometimes, if they're caught, but I'm too sharp for that."

"Then you don't know it makes God angry with you?"

"I never heerd tell of *Him*," said Tom. "I don't know no one who's angry 'cept the police. Nancy wasn't : she'd give me a real good supper if I'd took her home something worth having."

"Poor boy, you make me very sorry for you," said Mrs. Kelly ; but she looked across at little Mary, who sat listening in great astonishment, feeling that perhaps she had done an unwise thing in bringing such a boy as this to her home, even for a night or so.

"My little girl never heard any one talk so," she said, after a bit. "You won't do anything wrong and teach her, will you? or I must send you away."

Tom felt he shouldn't like that. "What !

don't she take nothing what isn't hers?" he asked, in a tone of unbelief.

"No, indeed; I hope she's been too well taught to do that: Mary's trying to please God, and do what He tells her."

"All right," said Tom, "I won't say nothing more about it; I don't want to learn the little girl no harm."

"There's a good boy," answered Mrs. Kelly; and then she began to talk of something else.

In spite of Tom's assurance that he wasn't hungry he made very short work of the bread and dripping, and looked round the room with a very contented face. Suddenly his eyes fixed on a crucifix which hung against the wall. "Lor!" he exclaimed, "whatever's he a-doing of that for?"

Both Mary and her mother turned round in the direction of Tom's gaze without exactly knowing what he was looking at.

"Him as is a-hanging up on that bit of wood," explained the boy.

Mrs. Kelly looked very grave. "I'll tell you all about it some day, Tom. That's what God did, Who came down and lived in the world, and was very poor, and then died on a cross just like that; we keep it there to remind us. Didn't you ever see one before?"

"No, that I never did!" cried Tom. "It's the first time I set eyes on such a thing."

"Well, I'm very glad you've seen it now," said Mrs. Kelly. "It's called a crucifix; shall you remember the name?"

Tom jerked his head by way of saying yes, and looked as if he would like to hear some more about it.

But Mrs. Kelly got up and began to wash the cups and clear the table, and then she and Mary went into a very small back kitchen and made up a bed there, which once was Joseph's, and when they came back Tom was still staring at the crucifix as if he could think of nothing else.

"There's some clothes that belonged to my poor boy," said Mrs. Kelly. "They're nothing very much, but they're better than yours. You're as near his size as can be, and you'd better put them on in the morning."

Tom nodded his head again, but even the prospect of new clothes could not take his thoughts from the crucifix. "I can't think why he come to do it," he said.   "Why, it must have hurt him worse than anything."

"Yes it did; but He liked to bear the pain because He did it for us—for you and me and Mary."

"No, he didn't do it for me," said Tom; "I didn't know him; I don't know nobody but them as lives up our court and round about."

"But He knew you, Tom, and He was thinking about you while He hung on a cross just like that."

Tom looked inclined to deny it, but he said nothing more.

"Well, now Mary and me are going to kneel down before that crucifix and say some prayers; suppose you kneel down too, and listen to what we say, and keep your eyes on the crucifix, and try and think how good it was of Jesus to hang there for you."

"Was that the name of Him?" Tom asked.

"Yes," said Mrs. Kelly, kneeling down with Mary by her side, and making the sign of the cross she began their usual night prayers.

Tom thought this all very strange, but he kept his eyes fixed on the crucifix and tried to listen. It seemed to him as if they were speaking to some one who had been very good to them, and he wondered who it was. Presently some words caught his ear which he could *quite* take in the meaning of—"Give us this day our daily bread." The poor ignorant boy thought it *must* be a fine thing to know some one who would do that; many a time he had wanted such a friend when he was standing at his crossing. But in a few seconds Mary and her mother got up, and Tom was sent to bed in the back kitchen: yet his last thoughts were of the crucifix, and he resolved to find out a little more about it next day.

Little Mary Kelly lay by her mother's side wide awake, though it was growing late.

"Mother, are you asleep?" she asked softly.

"No, child, but I soon shall be; I'm very sleepy."

"I only want to ask one thing, mother. Why don't Tom know any prayers?"

"Because he's never had any one to teach him. You'd best say a Hail Mary for him, dear."

"Yes, mother," said Mary, turning her face to the wall again. "I'll say prayers for him until he knows how;" and so she whispered a prayer to Christ's dear Mother for the poor crossing-sweeper, and shutting her eyes fell fast asleep.

It was still quite dusky when Mrs. Kelly with her little girl and Tom were getting breakfast, for she rose early and worked hard all day for her bread—sometimes getting a job of cooking or cleaning at gentlemen's houses, and doing a little washing at home between whiles. Times were hard then, for food and firing were dear, and Joseph's earnings had always been enough to clear the weekly rent, so it pressed heavily on the poor woman now; and yet she had not been afraid to take in this poor homeless boy, because she felt quite sure God would not let her miss what she gave him.

"I'm going out for half a day's work, Tom," she said, when breakfast was over, " and Mary goes to school; can I trust you to take care of the place till I come back, instead of locking it up as I mostly do ?"

Tom nodded : " All right," he said.

"You won't let in any street boys, will you, or get up to any mischief ? Remember, God's looking at you all the time, and He'll know everything you do ; God, Who came down here to be a man and die on the cross like that, you know, Tom ;" and Mrs. Kelly pointed to the crucifix.

" *That* can't see !" he said.

" No, that's only an image to remind us of Jesus Who did just like that when He was alive. He's up in heaven now, Tom, but He's quite near too, and He'll be watching you all day."

Tom looked in each corner of the room as if he expected to see some one there; however, he appeared to believe what he was told.

" All right," he said. " He shan't see me doing no harm, I'll promise you."

And the boy kept his word, staying quietly in till Mrs. Kelly returned ; spending the time in looking over some books with pictures they had left out for him, but gazing still more at the crucifix, as if he was yet wondering and thinking over all he had been told.

" What do you learn at your school ?" he asked Mary, when she came home again.

" Oh, ever so many things," said the child. " Reading and spelling and writing and needlework ; and then we sing, and then of course there's Catechism."

" Whatever's that there last thing you said ? I've heard of the rest, but I never heard of that."

" Oh, it's a little book which teaches us our religion : all about God, and what we've got to do and to believe.   The Sister asks the questions and we children say the answers."

" Whose sister ?—yours ?" inquired Tom.

" *The* Sister, I said ; the nun who teaches us. Sister Mary Agnes her name is."

" Lor ! do you mean to say one of them queer-looking women teaches you ?" cried Tom. " Why, I wonder you're not frightened ! I've seen a nun or two walking by sometimes, and me and a lot more boys calls after them and shouts.   It's such fun."

But Mary's little pale face was red now. "You naughty, bad boy; I'm sorry mother brought you here, that I am ; I'll ask her to send you right off if you behave so. Don't you know Jesus loves the nuns ? Why, they *belong* to Him, and you must make Him very sorry when you treat them badly."

Tom looked very grave then. "I'm sure I didn't know," he said. "I didn't know they belonged to anybody ; I only thought they dressed themselves precious queer. I'll never laugh at 'em again, Mary, if you like them so."

But Mary could not get over it at all that day,

and she began to wish Tom had never come, only he hoped he would learn better.

That night the boy knelt down with them before the crucifix without feeling quite so puzzled; he was listening for the words that had struck him so the night before, and at last they came, and Tom said out with the others, "Give us this day our daily bread," for he thought he should be sure not to be hungry any more if he asked for that.

"Mother," said Mary, when she was going to bed, "don't you think Tom ought to learn his Catechism?"

"Yes, I mean to teach him a bit when I get a chance, and we must get him to go to school and to church, if he stays here."

"Oh, let him stay, mother," said Mary, forgetting all about her anger and the nuns. "I'm sure he's not such a bad boy, and he'll never learn any better if he goes away. Couldn't I tell him some of the things that's in the Catechism, mother?"

"Yes, I believe you could, dear. The Sister's taught you so nicely, I should think you might teach Tom what you learn yourself."

"Then I'll begin to-morrow," said Mary.

Next day was a holiday at the school, being

Saturday, so at the first opportunity Mary drew near to where Tom was sitting cutting up firewood, with her Catechism in hand.

"Tom, if you like I'll teach you a bit," she said.

"All right," answered Tom ; "go ahead."

"Yes, but you'll listen and try and understand, won't you ? You'd like to save your soul, Tom, and go to heaven, wouldn't you ?"

"I don't know nothing about that, but I'd like to please you, anyhow," said Tom.

"Well then we'll begin. Now you can answer the first question, I'm sure."

"Who made you ?"

"Who made you," repeated Tom.

"Yes, but that's the question. You are not to say it after me, but tell me the answer."

"So I will if I knows what it is," said Tom.

"It's only to say who *did* make you, Tom. You know that."

Tom burst out laughing. "Well, if that ain't the queerest thing I ever heard. I s'pose I was made same as every one else, wasn't I ?"

"Yes, of course God made us all. You should just say, ' God,' Tom ; that's the answer."

"Well, I never knowed it afore," explained Tom.

But Mary shut her Catechism in despair and rushed to her mother.

"Oh, mother, I meant to teach him all I'd learnt, and he's so stupid he doesn't understand how to answer at all. He says he didn't know God made him, mother!"

"Very likely he didn't, poor lad," said Mrs. Kelly,   no way surprised at Tom's ignorance.

"It will all come in time, Mary, but you must have patience. They'll be able to teach him his Catechism if we can get him to go to school. Suppose you talk to him and tell him anything he wants to know; and I'd teach him the Hail Mary, if I was you, and our dear Lady will help him to understand all the rest."

So Mary went back to her pupil, and after trying a good many days she got him to learn the Hail Mary sufficiently well to join them in saying it at night and morning prayers.

"I don't clearly see the good of it, though," he said, when his little teacher declared he could say it quite well.

"Well, I'll tell you," said Mary, smoothing down her pinafore with both hands. "It's a prayer to Our Lady, the Mother of Jesus Who hung on the cross. Her name was Mary."

"Same as yours," put in Tom.

"Yes, Tom, I'm called after her because I want to be a little bit like her. Now, Tom, please listen. Of course we love Mary very much because Jesus loved her so dearly, and now she is up in heaven with Him He listens to all she asks for, and so if we get her to pray for us He's quite certain to do what she wants Him to."

Tom nodded his head. "I see," he said; "then if we ask Him things ourselves He won't do them 'cept for her?"

"Oh yes, Tom, indeed He does all we ask if it's good for us, only He likes His dear Mother to be asking at the same time, and I think He listens with a deal more pleasure when we pray and she prays too."

"*She* didn't hang on the cross, I s'pose," said Tom presently.

"No, but she knelt close by all the while, and saw her dear Son bearing all the pain, and it would almost have broken her heart, only she knew it was the way we'd get our sins washed away, so she was willing to bear it. So you see how much she loves us, Tom,"

"Yes," said Tom, "I see all that quite plain like; it's fine to hear you talk, Mary; go on a bit more."

"Oh, I can't tell you much, Tom, for I'm so little; I can only say what I've learnt; but the priest will tell you all you want to know, if you like."

Tom whistled and looked grave.   "I don't know; I've heard about them priests, and I don't much fancy them."

"But if Jesus were here now you'd like Him, Tom; you'd like to go and hear Him speak and teach ?"

"Yes, that I should; I'd go ever so far just to get a sight of Him and ask Him to make it all plain to me.   That's different to them priests."

"No, it's just exactly the same," said Mary quickly.   "Jesus knew we'd want some one to help us when He had to go away, and so He left the priests here, and made them able to do all that we should want, to teach us how to be good and to forgive us our sins ; and Jesus tells them what to say to us, Tom."

"Come now, I ain't a-going to believe all that," said Tom.   "That's *too* strong, that is."

"You *must* believe it," said Mary, getting very earnest; "Jesus said so, and it must be true. You wouldn't have seen Him die on the cross, and then go away and say you wouldn't believe what He told you, surely, Tom?"

"No, that'd be real mean," answered Tom. "If I *heard* Him say all that it'd be all very well, but you see I didn't."

"No, but other people did, and you must take their word. You didn't see Jesus die on the cross, but you believe He did it, don't you, Tom?"

Tom was caught then. "Yes, I do," he said at last; "and I'll try and believe it all. Suppose I go and kneel down before that image under the crucifix—her as you call Our Blessed Lady—and say the Hail Mary you've taught me, do you suppose she'll hear me a-doing of it, and pray for me too that I may believe it all?"

"Of course she will, Tom—come on."

So Mary and the rough ignorant boy knelt side by side before the little figure, and surely the dear Mother to whom they prayed looked down with love and tenderness upon them then.

"I think it's done me good," said Tom, getting up. "I'll do it again by-and-by, and perhaps I'll begin to understand it all after a bit."

A few days had passed since the little crossing-sweeper had found a new home, when to Mrs. Kelly's great distress he announced his intention one morning of going away. " 'Tain't that I don't like you," he said; "I'd like to stop always, but I ain't a-going to live out of you; it ain't fair. So I'll take my broom and do as best I can at my crossing, and maybe you'd let me come once in a while to see you and Mary and learn a bit more."

" Oh, Tom, you mustn't go !" cried Mary, and Mrs. Kelly was equally determined not to part with him.

" I can't let you go sweeping crossings now you live here, Tom," she said. " I don't want you to play in the streets; but I'm asking all about to see if I can't find anything decent for you to do, only you must have a bit of patience."

"But I'm a-living out of you, and that's what I don't want to," said Tom.

" But you help me, Tom. Who's to carry water and fill the kettle and light the fire, and take care of the place when Mary's at school and I'm out at work ? You be a good boy and go on behaving quietly here, and you'll get on finely by-and-by, I know."

So Tom said no more, but the thought remained in his mind, though he kept it secretly there, meanwhile filling up his time by doing

anything that came in his way to help. After a
bit he got employment from a greengrocer in the
next street, who sent him errands on Saturdays,
when he had extra business, and after finding he
could be trusted, began to give him work for a
few hours every day; and then Tom was happy,
for he felt he was earning something.

Meantime he was slowly beginning to understand what Mrs. Kelly and Mary tried to teach;
he had very quickly got to know the Our Father,
and they had succeeded in making him feel that
there was a God Who was angry when he was
dishonest and wicked, Who saw all that he did
by day or night.

The first Sunday Tom was with the Kellys
they could not persuade him to go to church,
but after that he always went, although at first
he was very much astonished at what he saw
and heard.

"Mary, Mary," he had whispered the first
Sunday morning he had gone to Mass, "is that
there image meant for Our Lady, same as yours
at home?"

Mary nodded her head. "Yes, Tom, only it's
larger."

"What's all them flowers and ca ndles for?"

But Mary would not say any more then. "I'll tell you after; please don't talk, Tom; say your beads and try and think that Jesus is going to offer Himself to God for our sins."

So Tom was silent, although many a time he wanted dreadfully to ask some question; however, he tried hard to keep saying Our Fathers and Hail Marys on the beads, as Mary with great difficulty had taught him to do.

When Mass was over and they were going home, Mrs. Kelly asked Tom what he thought of it all.

"It was wonderful," he said, drawing a deep breath. "I never did see such a lot of candles alight afore; I tried to say them beads as Mary told me, but I couldn't manage it very well because of them candles and flowers."

"You wanted to know what they were for, I suppose," said Mrs. Kelly. "When you understand, you'll find they help you to say your prayers better instead of hindering you."

Tom looked puzzled again.

"You know why we have an image of our dear Lady, don't you?"

"Oh yes, 'cause she was the Mother of Our Lord, and so we love her, and looking at the image makes us think of her up in heaven. Mary told me that."

" Yes; so we put flowers and candles at her feet, all to be little proofs of our love, to show her how we would like to give her everything sweet and beautiful if she was in the world now."

" I never thought of that," said Tom. "Why, of course I can look at the flowers and say Hail Marys at the same time. It's a pity I didn't know that afore I went to church."

"Well, then you saw lights and flowers on the altar, where the priest stood, didn't you, Tom ?"

" Heaps of 'em," answered the boy.

" That was because Jesus was there. No, you didn't see Him," she added, noticing Tom's surprised face. " He does not choose to let us see Him looking as He did when He lived in the world; but He is there just the same, only He allows Himself to look like a little bread and wine, but it is really Jesus, Tom—can you believe it ?"

" Yes," said the boy. " I suppose He's said it, and He knows better than me. Oh yes, I mean to believe all He's said."

" I am so glad," said Mrs. Kelly. " If you only do that, Tom, you will be so safe and happy, because then you will try and do what Our Lord tells you."

"I am a-trying; I ain't prigged anything since you told me it made Him sorry," said Tom.

"And He has seen you trying, and it has made Him love you very much, and He wants to forgive you all the sins you ever did against Him."

"I'm glad of it," remarked Tom. "There's a precious lot of 'em."

"Well, you'd best let me take you to see the priest to-night, and he'll talk to you and teach you better than me or Mary."

So Tom agreed, and from that time he went regularly to school in the week-days and to church on Sunday, and was gradually learning all of which he had been so ignorant a little while before.

"Oh, mother, ain't you glad you brought Tom home?" said Mary, one night. "Why, he's been to confession to-day, and got all his terrible sins forgiven, and it's so nice to know he's been baptised and made a Christian. I shall keep on saying a Hail Mary for him every night, for I'm sure Our Lady has been praying for him ever so."

Days and weeks went by, and though Tom Rogers said nothing, the old idea was still working in his mind, and he felt that he ought to be doing something more for himself instead of being a burden to Mrs. Kelly, who had hard work to support herself and child.

But it wasn't easy to get employment there in London, where there were so many boys who could do far more than he, and Tom did not know how to set about finding any work which would bring him in more wages than he had for running errands for the greengrocer.

At last a bright thought struck him : why shouldn't he go to sea ? He had heard a boy talking about it once, and saying what a fine thing it was, and that they were often glad to get hold of strong boys when a ship was sailing. The worst was it was such a long, long way to the sea, and Tom had no idea that a vessel could be found there in London.

One day he confided his wish to Mary, when they were watching together at the window for Mrs. Kelly to come home. "I say, Mary," he said, " wouldn't it be a fine thing if I went to sea ?"

" No," replied Mary. " I shouldn't like it at all ; but they wouldn't have you, Tom."

"I'd bring you home a parrot, and some shells, and some gold, and a lot of things," said Tom, who had not a very clear notion of geography, but imagined these things were to be found in every place he might sail to.

Mary laughed. She had no idea he meant it seriously, and then Mrs. Kelly came in, so no more was said about it.

But Tom did not forget, although perhaps he would not have carried out his plan but for some words which happened to catch his ear one day.

"Poor Mrs. Kelly," said one of the neighbours as Tom passed by; "it's a shame to have a great lad like that on her hands, and she a widow; working so hard too for her bread."

Tom did not hear any more, but his resolution was taken; he would go away without saying anything, and then they would get on better without him to keep in food and clothes.

So one morning, when Mary was at school and Mrs. Kelly out, Tom packed up a few things in a bundle, and giving one last look round the room went quietly out, feeling very, very sad, for he thought he should never see the kitchen again where he had been so happy and so kindly treated. He had got a little crucifix and a medal of his own safe in his jacket pocket; those were his only treasures to remind him of his friends when he was far away.

Tom did not feel quite sure he was doing right in going away secretly like this, but he was so resolved not to be a burden any longer on Mrs. Kelly, and so sure that she would not let him leave if he asked, that he felt this was his only chance of carrying out his plan ; yet when he thought of Mary missing him, and her mother thinking him ungrateful, his heart was very full.

However, he determined to find some way of letting them know why he had gone when he was fairly out of reach ; he couldn't bear them to think perhaps he was amongst bad companions and falling into sinful habits again.

So Tom walked on and on, though he did not know which way to take, and after some hours he found himself getting quite into the country, leaving streets and houses far behind.

He was hungry then, but he had brought with him what Mrs. Kelly had left out for his dinner, so he sat down under a hedge to eat it, thinking of Mary, and wondering if she was home and had found him gone yet.

After resting awhile he went on again, until

after a bit a good-natured woman gave him a lift in her cart, and hearing his story gave him some straw for a bed in her barn, and a good breakfast of bread and milk before he started again.   Tom found everybody kind to him, and so he managed to get along, asking his way from village to village, until he reached the sea, after a journey of several days.   When he got there his courage gave way, for it was night and he was tired and hungry, and people looked coldly at him, not speaking kindly as they did in the villages he had passed through ; so at last he went to sleep on a doorstep, just as he had often done in his old miserable life, waking in the morning from confused dreams of Mrs. Kelly, Mary, and Bouncer.

A woman had given him two pennies the day before, and with these Tom got some breakfast very early in the morning, at a dirty little shop he happened to find, and then, feeling better and braver, he went down to the harbour to look at the shipping.

There was a perfect forest of masts—vessels of all sizes ; and the boy's spirits rose at the sight, for surely he would find some one to take him from amongst so many !

While he stood gazing wistfully, a gentleman who had been watching his face touched his shoulder. " Are you a stranger here, my lad, or are you looking for somebody ?"

" I'm a-looking for somebody as 'll take me a-board one of them ships and make a sailor of me," said Tom, looking up into the good-natured face.

" Where's your father and mother, boy ?"

" Ain't got any: I lived with a woman who was kind to me, but she's hard work to keep herself, so I'm going to sea."

" How do you know you'll like it ?"

" I know I'll like it; I can tell by the very looks of it."

The gentleman laughed. " How would you like to have a voyage with me ? Yonder's my ship, and we sail to-morrow morning."

" I'd like it uncommonly," said Tom, with glistening eyes.

" But there's no one to speak a good word for you. How am I to know you'll behave yourself? You'll get a good rope's-ending if you don't."

But Tom was in no way discouraged. " All right," he said, " I don't care as long as you'll take me."

" Well, come and see how you like the look of my ship, and then if you're in the same mind I'll give you a trial."

All Tom's fears and regrets were gone then, and he felt happier than perhaps he had done in all his life before, as he found himself standing on the deck of a real vessel, such as he had often tried to imagine.

Before many hours the sea was between him and the few friends he had, who were by that time so anxious and distressed about him, but Tom got a good-natured sailor to write a few words at his own dictation to Mrs. Kelly, and this letter was put into the post before the vessel sailed.

Poor little Mary was in terrible distress when she found her companion gone, and Mrs. Kelly walked about to look for him in all directions. If it had not happened that a neighbour had seen him start with his bundle, nothing would have convinced her he was not killed or run over; as it was she could only persist in saying they should hear something yet, there was too much good in the boy for him to go off for any bad reason.

Now of course everybody had something to

say. "Depend on it, Mrs. Kelly," exclaimed one, "you'll hear no more of him. It's always the way if you've been kind to any one; they go off when they've had all they want."

" Ah, I thought no good would come of it," said another. "You won't be for taking in street-boys again in a hurry, I'm thinking."

But in the face of all this Mrs. Kelly and Mary would think no harm of Tom, and they were not at all surprised when the postman brought a letter written in a scrawling man's hand, though the words, they could tell, were Tom's. This is what it said :—

"*Ship ' Alice.'*

" DEAR MOTHER AND MARY,—This comes hoping to find you quite well as it leaves me at present, only I couldn't stop to be a burden no longer, and I'm going to be a sailor, and come home in about a year with lots of money and Mary's parrot. So no more at present, from

" Yours affectionately,

" TOM."

Mary burst into a storm of crying, and Mrs. Kelly wiped her eyes with her apron.

" Oh, mother, it's dreadful!" sobbed the child.

3—2

"We won't see Tom for a year, and perhaps he'll be drowned and never come back."

"Don't be so silly, child," said her mother. "Can't our dear Lady watch over him at sea as well as ashore ? Tom will come home again, you'll see; bless him !"

Mrs. Kelly went round amongst her neighbours with the letter in her hand. "I said I knew we'd hear all about it," she exclaimed triumphantly. "He's gone away for fear of being a burden to me; I'm proud of that boy, that I am. He's worth a dozen of them that's been better brought up! If I thought any one had said a word to him about being a burden, I really don't think I could help giving them a bit of my mind;" and then the good-hearted woman went off to the priest at the church to show him the letter.

"Well, really, Mrs. Kelly, it may be the best thing for the boy after all; that love of the sea seems born in some lads—it's like water to young ducks. Still Tom ought not to have gone off like that; he never said a word to me."

"I only hope he will come safe home again, Father," said poor Mrs. Kelly. "If I only had known before this ship sailed, I'd have fetched him home if I'd walked every bit of the way."

The priest laughed as he rose to open the door for her. "You mustn't be down-hearted," he said. "You'll see Tom safe back in a year's time, if you pray to Our Blessed Lady to watch over him."

"That's just what I said to my little Mary, Father; she's fretting dreadfully. If he'd only gone in one of those boats which keep near shore, and only stop away a week or two, I think I could have borne it, but it's dreadful to think Tom's miles and miles away at sea," and Mrs. Kelly went home again to try and comfort Mary.

So the summer passed, and autumn was over, and then came winter with its storms of wind and rain, when Mrs. Kelly and her little girl shuddered as they thought of Tom tossing on the sea, perhaps in danger.

What a number of prayers went up to God and the Blessed Virgin, I could never tell you; but I *can* say that they were not in vain, for at the end of the year Tom Rogers came home safe and well.

He was so grown and improved that the neighbours scarcely knew him, and he had become a thorough sailor, and loved the sea as much as he had expected. And he had not forgotten his friends, for he had brought Mary her parrot, and a smart shawl for Mrs. Kelly, which she put on with the greatest delight to go to church next Sunday.

"You haven't forgotten your religion, have you, Tom?" she asked, that first evening they were together again.

Tom hesitated a minute and looked down. "No," he said slowly. "I've been precious near it, though; they were a bad lot in our ship, both out and home, and there was a deal of swearing and drinking; and I was near giving up many times, only somehow I thought of this," (and here Tom put his hand on the little crucifix he carried inside his jacket), "and then I couldn't do like the rest."

"I'm thankful you took that with you, Tom; but you shouldn't have gone away as you did. You never even got the priest's blessing."

Tom looked ashamed. "I know," he said. "It wasn't because I didn't care, though; I thought he'd stop me going to sea. But I'll go to confession to-morrow, and I'll try and do better next voyage."

"Don't talk to me of next voyages," said Mrs. Kelly. "Surely you've had enough of the sea now, and can settle down and work on shore."

But Tom couldn't hear of that: his whole heart was in a sailor's life, and he had already imagined himself getting on step by step until at last he should have saved money enough to own a ship himself. "And then I'll give you both a voyage," he said; but Mrs. Kelly did not care about that offer.

The time soon came when Tom was longing to start again, and when they saw how firm his resolution remained, no one opposed him; so with many tears Mrs. Kelly and Mary saw him go.

But this time he obtained a berth in a large steam-ship running between England and America, so that his passages would be short and frequent.

This was a great comfort to Mrs. Kelly. "It's all very well to keep to your own prayers, but I must say that it seems like running into temptation to choose a life where you can't get Mass month after month; now it will be different."

The last night before Tom started he had a talk with Mary, which she remembered long after.

"It makes a fellow thoughtful," he said, "going out in those winds and storms again: some of these times I might get wrecked, or have a fall overboard. One of our crew fell from the mast as we came home, and by the time they'd hauled him in he was quite dead."

"Oh, Tom, don't tell me such things, I can't bear them: I wish you weren't going."

"Nonsense," said Tom. "I suppose I'm as safe there as here. There won't nothing happen to me afore my time. But Mary," and here the boy looked graver,—"*suppose* anything happened to me, do you think I'd be all right?'

"All right?" asked the child, not quite comprehending.

"Yes, you know I can't get to confession except on shore; suppose a storm or anything happened all of a sudden like, would God forgive me my sins without going to the priest?"

"Oh, yes, Tom; I've been taught all about that ever so long ago. You see, God expects us to go and tell our sins if we want Him to pardon us, but if there was no priest near you couldn't, and God is too good to punish us for what we can't help. If you'd look at your crucifix, Tom, and try and feel very, very sorry, and say the names of Jesus and Mary, I'm quite certain God would forgive you."

" I'm glad of that; I felt pretty sure I'd heard so myself, only I thought I'd make certain and ask you," said Tom.

But a great fear rose iu Mary's mind after that. "You don't think you're not going to come home again, Tom, do you ?" she said anxiously.

" No, of course not," he answered, trying to laugh away her fear. "Don't I tell you I'm going to make lots of voyages until I've earned money enough to buy a ship of my own. What shall I bring you from America, Mary ?"

"Oh, I don't care for anything, I don't want anything, if you'll only come back quite safe, Tom," and with that Mary burst into tears, and could not be comforted for a long time, even by her mother.

Next day they parted, and Tom, as he looked back to wave his hand, had a strange feeling in his heart as if he was looking at those two faces for the last time, and he could not help wondering why it was.

" One good thing is, he won't be away long,"

said Mrs. Kelly, turning from the doorstep and wiping her eyes with her apron, as if she felt the time for crying was past when Tom was clear out of sight; but poor little Mary fretted all that day and many more, for that last conversation had left a very unhappy feeling in her mind. Then, more than ever, she prayed to the Blessed Virgin to keep Tom safe, and to help him to be good amidst all the temptations which might be around him.

Before the boy had started he had told the priest how all the sailors had laughed at him for bringing his crucifix and caring for the medals which he always wore, and how once or twice he had been near throwing them away so as to escape the ridicule. And then the priest had bidden him try and be like Jesus, Who bore so much greater contempt without saying a word in complaint, and he encouraged Tom to try to help some of those around him to understand his religion.

"I'll try, Father," Tom had said. "I know it won't come easy, but I'll see what I can do, and anyway they shan't laugh me out of my crucifix and my prayers."

So the vessel sailed with every chance of a

good voyage, and everything went well with them until they started for the return passage. Then, before they had been out of port three days, they were overtaken by a fearful gale, and though it was a fine vessel every one on board felt the greatest alarm : even the captain and crew looked pale and anxious.

Tom was frightened too, but he kept saying his beads and begging pardon of God for all the sins of his life, and so he grew calmer.

There was a little child on board belonging to the captain, who had always taken a great fancy to Tom; now she came shivering and sobbing : "I don't want to be drowned, I want to go home to mamma."

"Hush, missy," said Tom. "Don't cry—that's no good. Here, take a look at this," and he pulled out his crucifix. "See, that's what Jesus did, because He loved you. He was in as bad a storm as this once, but He made the waves still all in a moment : let us ask Him to do it again now."

"I can't," said the child, clinging closer to the boy. "I forget my prayers now I'm so frightened."

"Say just a Hail Mary," said Tom.

"I don't know it; you say it, Tom! oh, be quick, pray quick!" she shrieked as another huge wave struck the vessel, shaking it from stem to stern.

The captain came by to look for the child, and caught her up all soaked and shivering. "Tom, Tom, where is he?" she cried, looking round as her father carried her away; but the sailor-boy was missing—he had been washed over with the wave, and hours after they picked him up, cold and lifeless of course, but his rosary twisted firmly round his fingers and his crucifix still safe against his breast.

The storm had abated then, there was every chance of getting safely home, and all were rejoicing, but the news of Tom's death cast a shadow over them all, for they remembered him kneeling and praying so fervently during the danger, and there were some who said their safety was God's answer to those prayers.

All this time Mary and Mrs. Kelly were looking forward hopefully to Tom's return. Never a day passed without his name being spoken many times, and every knock at the door brought the flush into Mary's cheeks, as she almost fancied it might be him come home unexpectedly.

So it was a terrible shock to the poor child when one day, after she had been on an errand for her mother, she found a stranger in the kitchen, at sight of whom she stopped short with her hand upon the door.

Then, as she took in the whole scene—her mother crying, the strange gentleman talking earnestly, and the crucifix Tom had taken to sea lying on the table, she understood it all, and with a bitter cry threw herself into her mother's arms, saying: " Oh, I know he's dead! I know he'll never come home!"

It was some time before Mary could listen quietly to what was said to her, but after a bit she dried her eyes and attended to what the stranger had to tell about Tom; how at the worst of the storm he was calm and quiet, praying all the time with a great trust in God, and that his rosary had been so firmly clasped round his hand that they had left it so when they put him in his rough coffin and left him to his grave at sea.

" Oh, mother, mother!" sobbed Mary, when they were alone again, "if only he had died at home, where we could have gone and looked at his grave sometimes, it wouldn't have seemed half so bad. I can't bear to think of him buried in the sea."

" But it was beautiful, Mary, to have him die so," said Mrs. Kelly. " We ought to be thankful about it, to know that he died with a prayer to our dear Lady on his lips. I think I never can feel glad enough that we saw him that night a poor little dirty boy crying on the doorstep."

" Yes, he'd never have learnt anything good but for that, would he, mother ?"

"Oh, yes, Mary, God meant him to learn, and so He'd sure to have found some way of making it come right. Only we ought to be very thankful God let us help."

"Don't you remember, mother, how he stared at the crucifix that night, and asked all kinds of questions ? And then I tried to teach him, but he didn't seem as if he could learn anything but the Hail Mary. That was the first prayer he said, mother. Wasn't it nice it should be the last ?"

And so they talked on of Tom and the old days as if they would never weary ; and the little crucifix, which had been brought back to them, was hung up as their greatest treasure.

Every one was sorry to hear the news : even those who had once felt a dislike to him because he was so poor and ignorant had all something kind to say, and promised to offer up prayers for his soul.

So poor Tom was not forgotten, and as years went by, and Mrs. Kelly grew old, and Mary was a woman and had little children of her own about her, they still loved nothing better than to talk of the cold winter evening when they had found him homeless and ignorant, and of God's goodness in letting them be the means of teaching him that faith and love to Jesus and His Blessed Mother which comforted him and saved him in his early death.

THE OLD PRAYER-BOOK.

CAN'T think how I lost it," exclaimed George Leslie, feeling in all his pockets, and turning them inside out, just as if that old well well-worn copy of the "Garden of the Soul" could have been hidden in a corner of the lining. "I wouldn't have parted with it for any money."

"What's the use of bothering about the old book ?" said the rest of the boys, who had been down in a party to their usual bathing-place behind the rocks, and now, as hungry as hounds, were not disposed to wait for breakfast just for the sake of hunting for what they thought so small a loss. "You've plenty more books, George, and if you haven't you can buy one."

"Yes, but I couldn't buy one to be the same as this," answered George. "There—suppose you fellows get on home, and I'll just run back and have a look for it; I'll catch up with you in no time;" and away he went to search about amongst the rocks where he had dressed after his bath, to no purpose, for there wasn't a book to be seen anywhere.

A little sun-burnt girl stood watching him curiously, and as George came up she asked him " if he'd lost anything;" but when he described the book, she shook her rough hair, and said, " 'Taint no manner of use your looking for it, master. I see Bill Stevens ferretting about there not five minutes ago; he's found it most like, and you'll never see it any more."

" Who's Bill Stevens ? and which way did he go ?" asked George.

" He lives about here; he's a fisherman," said the child, gravely. " Yonder he goes—see, right across there," and she pointed with one hand to the figure of a man, so far off across the shingly beach that evidently it was hopeless to think of catching up with him then.

So George Leslie went off rather sorrowfully, taking the way his companions had gone to the town. He was vexed to lose this old Prayer-Book, because it had been the last gift of his dead sister, on a day which was memorable to him—the day of his First Communion.

No sooner was the lad out of sight, than the little sun-burnt girl who had spoken to him, sat down behind the rocks, and laughed loudly; then she drew out of the folds of her ragged frock the old, worn book, and began turning over the leaves while she talked to herself.

"He seemed sorry—but *I'm* not sorry," she said. "I can't get books—and I like 'em. I wasn't a-going to give him this one. Didn't I tell him a fine tale?" and here she laughed again. "I don't know no Bill Stevens—not I. He'll never get his old book again."

Polly Edwards wasn't much of a scholar, but she had managed somehow to learn enough to make out words which were not over long; so she soon found that her treasure was not a book of tales, as she had hoped, and that it was something of the kind which she had seen the ladies and gentlemen who came to that place in the summer season, carry in their hands to church. After all, she was rather sorry for keeping it. Perhaps if she had told the young gentleman she'd found it, he would have paid her some money for giving it back to him !   Polly looked round, hoping to catch a glimpse of him, but he had evidently given up his old Prayer-Book for lost.   So she must keep it now, and away she ran homeward, to show what she had got to her mother.

On her way, Polly met her brother Ned going "winkling," as the sea-side children call it, so she went with him, and sat down on the beach, while Ned gathered his periwinkles on the rocks; and having nothing better to do, she opened her old book, and read the words which were written in rather faded ink on the fly-leaf. "George Leslie, from his sister, on the day of his first—" But there Polly stuck fast, for, as I have told you, she wasn't a fine reader, and the long word which came next was too much for her.

"Ned, Ned !" she cried, "what word begins with C O M ?"

Ned was older than Polly, and he had once been for nearly a year at the school in that village. "C O M ? Why, it's *coming*, I s'pose, Polly."

"No, it isn't," answered the girl; "it's ever so much longer. There's another *m* comes next, and a lot more letters,"

Ned stood still on the rocks, and thought a minute. " What's the book about, Polly ?"

"Oh, I don't know. I don't think it's nice ; it's a book to take to church, Ned, and I found it on the rocks. *Don't* you know if there's any word begins with—a C and an O and two Ms, Ned ?"

" A book to take to church," repeated Ned. " C and O and two Ms—whatever can it be ? Just wait a minute, Polly, and I'll take a look ;" and Ned bounded off the rock, and bent over the old Prayer-Book with the air of one who knew all about it. "Oh it's 'commandment,'" he said. " What a stupid I was, to be sure ; of course it must be commandment ; they always read 'em in church."

Polly never doubted Ned's knowledge, but she wanted to understand a little more about it. "And what's the meaning of it, Ned?" she asked. " What day is it his sister give him the book ?"

" I don't know," said Ned. " I s'pose he knew, and that was enough. I'm going home now, Polly. I guess I've found four or five quarts." So the children went home, and their " winkles " were left in salt water to get the sand out, and next day their mother boiled them and measured them, and Ned found he had four quarts to sell. That was *his* way of earning a few pence to help keep him.

"Where's father, mother?" asked Polly, as she watched the table being laid, and the herrings and potatoes put on for dinner.

"Not home yet," said Mrs. Edwards, going to the door and looking out over the sea, anxiously. The big waves broke with a great noise on the beach, and the wind whistled dismally, and the mist was rising in the distance. "I wish he'd got home; we shall have a storm," said the fisherman's wife, and as she came back and helped the children to their dinner, she sighed heavily.

But the wind rose higher; it blew so loud you could hear nothing else except the dashing of the waves on the shore. Most of the boats were in, but not the one belonging to Polly's father, and it was two days later before the news came that he was drowned.

The neighbours were poor, and had children in numbers of their own, but they were ready to help the widow and her five boys and girls as much as they could. Mrs. Edwards talked at first of "going into the house," but they persuaded her that with her washing and a bit of sewing she'd get along ; and the children were getting big ; Ned earned a trifle by selling winkles, and Polly could mind the little ones at home.   So the poor woman tried to struggle on, and then some of the gentlemen's families staying there made up a subscription which put them all in mourning, and gave them a fair start.

" You'll have to help me now, Polly," said her mother. "You can't be playing on the rocks half your time, now your father's dead and gone and there's so little coming in ;" and Polly sighed and looked out longingly at the sea she loved so. It was very dull and tiresome to have the baby to drag about all day, and two more to mind beside.

What with her father's death, and all their troubles, Polly Edwards had almost forgotten the old Prayer-Book; but the first Sunday when she put on a black frock, she felt so unusually clean and respectable that she thought she should like to go to church, like she saw the ladies do, with her book in her hand.

Mrs. Edwards made no objection. " Yes, if you like, child, though what's the good of you going I don't know. Mind and behave yourself. Don't let the gentlefolks see you misbehaving when they've been helping us as they have."

Polly promised good conduct and went her way, and sat, and stood, and knelt like the rest during the service, with her eyes very widely opened all the time. As the congregation came out of church she stood quietly in the porch looking a model of good behaviour, with her Prayer-Book held fast; and many persons spoke kindly, knowing that she was one of the children of Joe Edwards, the fisherman, who had lost his life in a storm not a week before.

"And is that your Prayer-Book?" said one lady, stretching out her hand to take it, but when she opened it she started back with horror.

"How did you come by this, child? It's a horrid Papist book—a wicked book!"

Polly, quite frightened, hung down her head and burst into tears. "I only found it on the rocks," she whined. "I thought it was a book to bring to church; I didn't mean any harm."

"There, don't be frightened, child, I'm not scolding you," said the lady. "Of course you didn't know it was a bad book—but you mustn't keep it. Why did your mother let you have it?"

"She didn't know," said Polly, still half-crying. "I found it the same day as father died that night, and mother's been busy, and I hadn't

showed it her. 'Tisn't her fault," added the
child, afraid of offending one of the "gentlefolks" who had helped them.

All further talk was stopped by the clergyman
coming out of the church just then, and the lady
who was speaking to Polly turned round to him
with the objectionable Prayer-Book in her hand.

"Oh, Mr. Fairburn, I am so glad you are here!
Do you know I have actually found one of poor
Edwards's children with a Roman Catholic
prayer-book at our church."

The rector looked horrified, and held out his
hand for the old "Garden of the Soul," which he
opened and looked at while Polly explained
once more how it came into her possession.

"If you came regularly to the school, and
learned your duty, Polly Edwards," he said
severely, "you would know better than to keep
a book like this. I must talk to your mother
about you."

Polly flew home then—glad to get free. Certainly she had lost her book, for Mr. Fairburn
had put it into his pocket; but she did not mind
so much, only she was sorry now she had taken
it—"George Leslie" might as well have had it
after all——!

Poor old Prayer-Book!   It went home in the clergyman's pocket to his comfortable rectory and there was handed over to one of his servants with the request that she would immediately burn it in the kitchen fire; but, instead of following out her master's order directly. she put it on the dresser, with the intention of seeing what book it was when she had leisure, and there it was found by Lucy Robson, the young girl who had only lately lived there as housemaid.

How it was she came into the kitchen then, or happened to notice the soiled old Prayer-Book, Lucy could never tell; but later, she always said that God and her good Angel had chosen that way to save her from the path she had entered on, and that it was a blessed day for her when the "Garden of the Soul" was brought into the clergyman's house. Still, when she opened it so carelessly, and saw such long-familiar words, it was closed and flung aside half angrily, half timidly.

The writing on the fly-leaf had caught Lucy Robson's eye as it had the little ignorant fisherman's girl; but the long word that had puzzled Polly Edwards and her brother Ned, was not strange to one who had been trained from a baby

to know and think of a " First Communion "
as a day of joy and gladness that could come but
once in a long lifetime. Next minute Lucy
picked up the book from the floor where it had
fallen, and slipping it into her pocket went
about her usual work.

There was a strange flush on her cheek during
the day, and she was absent and forgetful ; but
all this was nothing to the confusion in her
mind, which made it so hard to remember she
was now a servant in a Protestant clergyman's
house, acting a false part—the part of Judas,
who deceived his Master. It seemed as if the
last three years were all a horrid dream, and she
was once again at home, a girl in the Catholic
school of the London church where she had
been baptized and confirmed, where she had
again and again received the pardon of her
childish sins, and knelt at the altar for the
coming of Jesus in Holy Communion.

But when it was evening—when the other
servants were at church, and Lucy, whose place
it was to stay in then, sat down alone to turn
over the leaves of the old Prayer-Book, the
three years of her deception, of the denial of
her faith, were no dream any longer—she saw

their real, actual sin so plainly. From one page to another she turned—all condemned her. The morning and night prayers, ah, how long since she used them !—the devotions for Mass —Mass which she had neglected and turned from; confession—the confession which she had given up first before she began to go away from the faith of her childhood;—all, all reproached her ! There was no comfort for Lucy Robson in the old Prayer-Book : and so she closed it and sat with it on her lap, gazing into the fire. Once or twice she thought she would throw it there, see it burn, and so get away from the misery of self-reproach which had come through it, but it was more than the girl dared do. One minute she held it near the flame, but the next it was on her knee again, with her head resting upon it, and tears falling fast on its faded cover.

What could she do ? Pray ? Ah, no ! God was offended; Jesus, the merciful Saviour, grieved; Mary, His Blessed Mother, even could not love or listen to her now, so Lucy told herself; and yet at last, after a long time, she opened the old Prayer-Book at the well-remembered Act of Contrition and said it more than once. There was no distinct purpose for the future in the girl's mind, no positive plan for returning to her religion, but one thing she was sure of, that with her whole heart she repented the past and wished that it had never been.

We must go back three years, and see Lucy Robson in her home, trying to gain her mother's consent to her going away to service.

Mrs. Robson was poor, but a tidy, respectable Catholic woman, and knowing Lucy's light, thoughtless nature, she had set herself resolutely to oppose this wish to leave home.

Certainly the girl was fifteen years of age, and many not so old were at work. If only she could hear of a place there in London, where Lucy could be under her own eye, she would be glad to get her out ; but to go into the country, away from all her friends, was quite another thing, the mother said, as she declared she " would not hear of it."

Lucy was very vexed about it,—she was "sick of stopping at home," she said. "It was such a bother to be the eldest of so many children, and have to help with them all day ; she didn't mind work, but she wanted to get away, she wanted a change."

So when, through a girl whom she was acquainted with, Lucy heard of a lady who wanted a young person as servant, some miles in the country, she was determined to go, if she could only get her mother's consent; and when she did *not* get it, she turned sullen and lazy and altogether disagreeable.

"I wonder you're not ashamed of yourself," Mrs. Robson would say; "a great girl your age doing nothing, when I'm working hard from morning till night. Why, Fanny, who's four years younger, is worth two of you."

"Let me go to service, and I'll work, mother. I'm tired of home," was the answer.

Poor Mrs. Robson! She fretted a good deal about her eldest girl just then; it was a long time before she could make up her mind to tell the priest how anxious she was, but at last she begged him to "give Lucy a talking to, for there was no doing anything with her."

Father Hall tried his best to lead the girl to be obedient and useful at home; but she had no intention of following his advice, and grumbled about his being "strict" and "cross" and was more anxious than ever to get away among strangers, where she should do more as she liked, and not be talked to and lectured as if she was a child,—she, a girl of fifteen !

So winter came on, and Lucy's father was out of work week after week, and things were desperately hard, and it was certain that they must get the eldest children out into the world to help. So Fred went to a place in a tradesman's family, and Lucy was allowed to look for a situation too. She had lost the one which had been offered her, of course, but being tall, pleasant-looking, and well mannered, she soon got engaged in a respectable family, where she was to help the elder servants and make herself useful in any way she could.

" Are they Catholics ?" the priest had asked, when Lucy, by her mother's desire, told him she had found a place.

" Well, no; they are not," she answered, " but I have asked leave to go to Mass, and have been promised to do so every Sunday."

So Father Hall gave her a little advice as to the need there was she should take care of her Faith, and be very regular in her duties. And her mother begged her to be a good girl, and meet her at Mass on Sunday mornings; and so Lucy left home in high spirits, as full of self-trust as she could possibly be.

For a little while all went well, it seemed, but it was *only* for a little. Before three months had gone, every one could see what a change had come over Lucy Robson, how bold her manner had grown, and how she loved to show herself dressed out in rubbishing tawdry finery.

" Do for goodness sake come neat and respectable to Mass, child," Mrs. Robson would say, as they walked part of the way from church together.   "I declare I'm ashamed to see you with such a bonnet perched on your head and ribbons a-flying like that. What's come to you, Lucy ?"

Then Lucy would toss her head and say, "Lor, mother, what a fuss you do make. *Every one* dresses so, and you can't expect me to look as if I came out of the Ark. I'm sure it isn't much I spend with only £8 a-year wages."

" That's just it, Lucy ; if you were trying to get decent things about you, you'd have nothing to spend on ribbons and finery."

Then Lucy went back to her place more determined than ever to do as she liked ; and after a little while she began to spend the time allowed her for Sunday Mass in taking a walk with acquaintances who put more foolish, wrong thoughts into her head than were there already.

For a long time Lucy had been accustomed to go to her confession and Communion every month. When she was at home I suppose nothing would have induced her to let the usual time go by without it, but in place it was very different.

Her mistress would have made no difficulty; Lucy had not even the excuse for her neglect of being hindered and ridiculed; it was her own fault, her own wilfulness which kept her from the sacraments; and she began to feel her religion was a troublesome one, which cost her more sacrifices than she was ready to make. There was no thought in her heart just now of giving it up—that time had not come; no, she would go to her duties at Easter—she wasn't *obliged* to do more, and surely that was enough for her; and Mass—well, she must go to Mass, of course; she had missed once or twice, but she wouldn't miss any more if she could help it!

That was the way of things with Lucy Robson, when, one day, the cook where she lived had a friend come to see her from the country, who said, amongst other things, that she knew of a nice place for a girl who wanted to be house-maid; it was a good family—a clergyman's family, and they gave good wages, but they wanted a young servant who would "learn their ways."

Lucy had kept one wish in her mind for a long time—the wish to get away at the first opportunity, to be more at liberty and not know that her mother was watching her so narrowly ; so as she listened, a great desire came to get this situation which was spoken of, and she asked if there was any chance for her, if she wrote about it.

" Oh ! I didn't know you were leaving," said the woman. " I should say you'd be just the girl for them."

So Lucy explained that she was not exactly leaving, but that she wanted to "better herself," and get more wages, to help her mother ; and the end was that she gave notice to her mistress, obtained the new place on trial, and kept her plans a secret from all her friends until a few days before she had to leave.

Then she walked into her mother's room quite late one evening, when she had only a few minutes to stay.

" Mother I'm changing my place," she said. "I'm going to a nice family, where I'll get more wages, and I'll be able to help you a bit. I've only three days before I go, but I'll look in again to say good-bye."

How the careless words and tone went to the mother's heart!

"Leaving your place, child," she said. "Why, what fault does your missis find?"

"None at all," said Lucy, with a toss of the head. "It's my own doing; I want to better myself."

"That's the way with girls nowadays," cried Mrs. Robson; "never satisfied, always talking of 'bettering' themselves. I wish I could see you do better in one way, Lucy; and that's in going regularly to your duties and keeping closer to your religion. Many's the night I'm kept awake thinking of you and praying for you."

Lucy laughed. "I'm all right, mother," she said. "You can't expect me to be as particular as if I was an old woman. But I can't stay; I'll come in before Thursday."

"Stop, child!" cried Mrs Robson. "Who knows anything of this place? I can't have you go away like that. Have you told Father Hall?"

Again Lucy tossed her head—Father Hall again! Must she never do anything without asking the priest?

"A friend of our cook's told me of it, mother; and it's a real good place. And I'm only going for a month on trial, so if it don't suit me I shan't stop."

"Are they Catholics, do you know?"

"No, they're not, mother," said Lucy, getting rather red. "I daresay there's a Catholic church near—of course there must be. But I can't stay now, mother," and away she went.

All that night poor Mrs. Robson lay awake, thinking of Lucy. What was to be done if she turned so wild and "masterful?" Next morning she called on the priest to tell him her anxiety.

"What is the name of the place?" he asked. "I will write to the priest, if there is one, and ask him to look after Lucy. That seems the only thing to be done, as she has engaged to go."

It had never struck Mrs. Robson before that Lucy had not named the place where she was starting to. "Why, bless my heart!" she exclaimed; "I'm losing my head, it seems. I clean forgot to ask her where it was, Father; for she flew in in such a hurry, that it quite gave me a turn."

Father Hall looked grave. "Send her to me before she goes," he said. "I should like to speak to her myself."

So when Lucy came in next time her mother told her what the priest had said, and the girl, now getting more and more apt in deception, promised to go to him that evening, and even parted with her mother early on the plea of having more time to go round by the church; and so with a hasty good-bye she was gone—but not to Father Hall—only to call in on another girl, as giddy as herself, to spend a few minutes in idle talk and laughter before she must go in.

And that was how Lucy Robson came into the Reverend Mr. Fairburn's family, where she was supposed to be a Protestant like the rest, where she went to the church every Sunday morning, and looked about her, and noticed the ladies' bonnets, and saw nothing to remind her of God, nothing to make her feel she was in His presence. And she tried to think she was happy, but there were still times when her heart was heavy and sad, when she would have given her life to get back the peace and the safety she had lost.

Father Hall knew, when he found where she was, that Lucy was miles and miles, from any Catholic church. He wrote to her, her mother wrote, begging and almost commanding her to return ; but in vain ; the girl declared that she was comfortable, and should stop where she was ; another time, if she could get a Catholic place, she would. After this letters grew fewer and fewer ; thoughts of home and God and duty came very very rarely, until that Sunday when the old Prayer-Book found its way into the clergyman's kitchen, and Lucy cried so bitterly over her falseness to her faith.

For many days she went about her work listlessly—unlike herself. The book was always in her pocket, but she had not opened it again ; where was the use ? She thought it only made her miserable. She couldn't alter things then ; some time she would. Ah, yes ! when she had stayed on longer, till she was old enough to take a good place in London, she would get right again — get amongst

Catholics once more, and be as good as any of them.

That resolve did not bring her much comfort, however; something seemed always urging her to get free now, to begin to break away from the chains she had made for herself, and return to God without delay. But still Lucy stifled her sense of right, and tried to go on as usual, looking at her old Prayer-Book on Sunday evenings, crying over it, and resolving to amend, and yet putting off the first step.

The matter of the old Catholic book had quite slipped out of the clergyman's mind, after he believed it had been burned according to his orders. He even forgot to give Mrs. Edwards the "talking-to," with which he had threatened Polly. But the girl often thought of the book, and wondered where it was, and whether Mr. Fairburn had read it, and whether he knew the meaning of the words which were written inside. Polly had found out now it was a Catholic book, and though she did not understand the meaning of the name "Catholic" at that time, it was treasured up in her mind, until years after, when she was far away from the little fishing village, and in a town where by God's blessing she learned to know and love the true faith which she found there. So the shabby copy of the "Garden of the Soul" in time brought a blessing to the little ignorant girl, whilst it was the means too of bringing Lucy Robson back to the religion of her childhood.

During the weeks which passed while she was so restless and unhappy, the summer had quite passed, and autumn had come. The little place was very empty of visitors now, and the few who were still left were talking of departure. How it was that, in the healthy seaport, a terribly infectious fever burst out, no one could ever tell; but it spread and spread amongst the poor, and reached the homes of the better classes, and at last it travelled to the rectory, and struck down the young servant, Lucy Robson. By the doctor's advice, to save the rest of the family, if possible, she was moved to the hospital in the town, some fifteen miles off, and there she had every care and the best nursing. Poor girl! she talked so pitifully in her unconsciousness; she called so imploringly for a priest and for her mother, that Mrs. Robson was sent for by Mr

Fairburn's orders, and on her arrival she went herself to the Catholic church there, to ask for some one to see Lucy. Day after day the priest paid his visit, risking his health and life so gladly in the hope of seeing some gleam of consciousness in which he might help that poor troubled soul. In broken sentences she talked of being "false," in half-intelligible words she spoke of her wish to "get right some day," and through all her illness nothing would induce her to part with the old Prayer-Book. At last the fever was gone; but the girl was sinking fast, for she had not strength to recover from the attack. The first time she recognised her mother, she hid her face in her pillow and cried bitterly, for that familiar face brought back memories of happier, better days, which well-nigh broke her heart to think of now. But gradually she was prepared to make her peace with God, and after receiving the grace of the sacraments she grew calmer and quieter. During the last few days she told the priest who attended her the story of the old Prayer-Book.

"Was it not strange, Father, that I should meet with it like that? If it had not happened, I am afraid to think what would have become of my soul." She did not know that the priest had read the inscription on the fly-leaf, and recognised in the name of "George Leslie" a young friend who was preparing for the priesthood in that very town.

"I should like to have this book," he said. "Not now—when you have done with it;" and Lucy knew that Father Gilbert was thinking of the time when she should need books and priests and sacraments no longer,—when death should have taken her away.

Very few were the days she lingered, and then the parting came. Life, which might have been used for God, was going fast, with all its neglected opportunities, with all its sins and unfaithfulness—forgiven, we know, by the pardon of God and the precious Blood of Christ poured out upon the soul in the sacrament of penance —but still to be judged, and to suffer for, before that soul could rest in the joy of heaven. Poor Lucy! She received the last sacraments, and passed away, breathing the names of Jesus and Mary, and then they laid her body in a grave in that strange town, with a small Cross to mark the spot; and her poor sorrowing mother went back to her home in London, to tell the younger children of their sister's death, and how her last messages to them were to beg them prize their Faith, and never be careless and false as she had been.

Then the old Prayer-Book found its way back to its first owner, and when he heard the history of Lucy Robson, from the lips of Father Gilbert, he thanked God with all his heart that he had once lost it and looked for it in vain on the rocks near the little seaport village, where it had done its work.

CHARLIE PEARSON'S MEDAL.

"NOW, my boy, will you wear this medal to remind you of to-day— the day you have been made God's child?" said the priest who had just baptised little Charlie Pearson, who stood in the sacristy of St. Anne's Church clutching his mother's shawl with one hand, and wiping his eyes with the back of the other.

"Say 'thank you' to the gentleman and make a bow, can't you?" exclaimed the woman, nudging Charlie with her elbow as she spoke, and so making things worse, for he burst into a regular roar then, and kept it up until he was safely out of the church and on the way home, with the bright medal squeezed tightly in his hand.

"Ain't you ashamed of yourself?—and

you nigh upon eight years old," Mrs Pearson began. "I wonder what the priest 'll think of you—he isn't used to see boys act like that, I know."

"I didn't like it," said Charlie, gulping down his sobs, and giving the last touch to his eyes with his jacket sleeve—for there was no reason to cry now. "What's he been a-doing of, mother ?"

"Well, he's made a Catholic of you," explained the mother. "You'll go to the school now at the church, like Pat and Barney Murphy, and it'll be a fine thing for you."

"Oh ! I'm a Catholic am I ?" said Charlie, slowly. "I didn't know that was what he did to me. What's the good of it, mother ?"

"Why, you'll be a better boy now, and not be saucy to your mother, and like your schooling, and all that," said Mrs. Pearson. "Catholic boys are better than others—or leastways ought to be."

"You're a Catholic, too, ain't you, mother ?" asked Charlie, looking up in her face.

"No, child, no; that's none of your business, I'm too old to learn new things ; it's very different to you. There, hold your tongue, do ;

for here's your father waiting at the door," and Mrs. Pearson hurried her steps, for she knew by her husband's face that he was out of temper.

"It's a fine thing to come home," said the man. "Go out early to work, come home to my dinner, and 'tisn't ready. Where've you been?"

"That's neither here nor there," replied his wife, who had a sharp answer always ready. "I'm come now, and it's only five minutes after twelve, and that's not much to grumble at."

Charlie had been waiting all this time to publish his news, and now, in spite of his mother's signs and frowns, he pulled out the medal.

"See, father, the parson up at the church yonder gave me this; and he put salt in my mouth, father, and poured a lot of water over me and——" But Charlie's tale was cut short by his father's fist coming down on the table with a force which made it shake, whilst a terrible curse fell from his lips as he turned on his wife, asking, "What she'd been a-doing to the boy?"

"Doing what I like," said Mrs. Pearson, not much daunted, for oaths were common things in that unhappy home. "It don't hurt you I s'pose, if the boy's christened, instead of growing up a heathen."

"Yes, it does!" shouted Pearson. "You've been taking him to the priest; you'd better out with it at once."

"Yes, I've took him to the priest," said Mrs. Pearson, looking her husband in the face; "and if I'd twenty boys, which thank God I haven't, I'd take them too—there now."

Charlie Pearson wasn't easily frightened, but the storm which followed made him shake all over, and before he knew anything, he was thrown roughly on the floor, his medal taken from him and tossed out of the window, and his father was gone, leaving his wife to pick up the bits of broken glass and crockery which he had smashed in his rage, scolding Charlie vigorously all the time.

"What need had you to say anything about it for?" she cried. "Didn't I tell you to hold your tongue? Couldn't you see your father was cross, without going and making him worse with your stupid chatter? He'll drink away all the money in his pocket now at 'The Crown '—thanks to you."

"I didn't mean any harm," sobbed Charlie. "Oh, dear, I wish I hadn't been made a Catholic, if this is what's to come of it." But here the door opened, and Mrs. Murphy, who . lived in the downstairs room, came in.

"Your master's a bit put out, isn't he ?" she said looking at Mrs. Pearson and Charlie, and then at the room.

"You may well say that, Mrs. Murphy, and him storming and breaking the cups and saucers I had before I married him, and knocking the boy down, and making a row as was nigh enough to bring in the neighbours ; and all because I've took your advice and had Charlie here christened a Catholic."

"Oh ! that was it, then ? Never you mind ; he'll get over it soon enough, I'll be bound."

"It's fine talking when you've got a steady, decent husband to work for you," said Mrs. Pearson. "However, the boy's christened, and all the storming and the swearing won't undo *that*."

"No, thank God !" said Mrs. Murphy. "And you'll never repent this day, take my word for it, Mrs. Pearson. The boy'll grow up to be a comfort to you."

"Well, it's to be hoped so, I want it bad enough. I can't think, either, why I've been so set on seeing him a Catholic, for I don't hold with them particularly myself. It's only seeing that they look after the boys a bit, instead . of leaving them to chance, made me take Charlie. He's all I've got since the little ones died, and I'd like him to grow up respectable."

Charlie had recovered himself by now, and told Mrs. Murphy of his medal, and what had become of it.

"Sent it out of the window, you say?" cried the woman. "Go down and look for it this minute, and don't give up till you find it. It's been blessed, you may be sure, and you don't know the good it'll do if you wear it."

So Charlie ran down into the street, and after a long search, in which he had the help of all the dirty urchins round, the medal was discovered; and being rubbed bright again with the corner of Mrs. Pearson's apron, it was tied on a piece of tape round the boy's neck.

"Father shan't get hold of it again," he said. "I'll keep it safe now I've found it."

"Ay, do," answered his mother. "I can't rightly see the use of it, but maybe you'll find out after a bit. It's sure to mean *something*, else the priest wouldn't have given it you."

Many a time that day, as he played in the street or sat on the doorstep, Charlie pulled out the little medal, to make sure he had it safe, and to turn it over and over in his dirty hands, trying to make out what was written on it. At last he called out to Pat Murphy, "I say, Pat, I want you."

"What's up?" said Pat, looking round the doorway of his mother's kitchen.

"See here—this is my medal! What's it all about?"

"Oh! I've got one too; so 's Barney. It's a medal of the Blessed Virgin."

"What's that?" asked Charlie.

"Don't you know that much? Well you *are* a young stupid," answered Pat, scornfully. "They'll teach you all that if you come to our school," and away he went. It was rather shabby of him to leave poor ignorant Charlie so, but the fact was Pat didn't want to be let in for an explanation!

Presently Charlie Pearson went back to his

mother. "Mother, I want to go to the Catholic school, where Pat and Barney go. May I?"

Mrs. Pearson was very busy washing by that time, and in no mood to listen to Charlie. "Don't come bothering me, boy. I've had you christened, and that's enough for one day. Get out of the way, can't you?"

So the boy went back to his seat on the doorstep, with a listless, weary face. But all in a minute it brightened, for at the sound of a quick step passing by, he looked down the street, and saw the well-remembered face of the priest who had baptized him in the morning; and without stopping to think twice, Charlie ran after him and greeted him as an old acquaintance.

For a minute Father Bernard looked puzzled. "Well, what little boy are you?" he said. "I don't know you, do I?"

Charlie felt almost injured at being so soon forgotten. "I'm him as you christened down at the church this morning."

"Oh! I remember quite well now. Yes, you cried, and were too frightened to say good-bye to me. How was that, and you're not afraid now?"

"Why *here's* different," answered Charlie, rather at a loss how to explain that to see the priest in church for the first time, and to meet him there in his own street, was not at all the same thing.

Father Bernard smiled. "I'm glad you are not so foolish now—you won't be frightened any more, I'm sure. So you live here, do you ? I must call on your mother some day, and ask her to send you to school."

"I'd like that, I think," said Charlie. "I asked her to-day if she'd let me, but she only told me to get out of her way."

"I daresay you are in her way very often, so you would be better at school. Besides, a boy your age ought to be learning, and you have so much to learn, too, now you're a Catholic."

"I want to learn about this," said Charlie, bringing out his medal. "I'd like to know what's the good of it, and what the writing means that's on it."

All this time Father Bernard had been walking towards home, while Charlie kept trotting at his side. They were just at the church then, and the priest stopped.

"I could hardly make it quite plain to you,

my boy, just in a moment, I fear.   It is a medal
of the Blessed Virgin.   Do you know who I
mean ?"

Charlie shook his head.

" Do you know who I mean by Jesus Christ ?"

" Oh, yes—I went to the Protestant school on
Sundays for a bit, and I heard of *Him* there.
Him as was born on Christmas Day, you mean ?"

" Yes.   Well, the Blessed Virgin was the
Mother of that same Jesus Christ, and because
of this we ought to love her very much."

" But what's the good of the medal ?" said
Charlie.

" The 'good' of it is to remind us of her.
When Christ was dying, He gave us His Mother
to love for His sake ; and now she is in heaven
with Him we love her still, and if we want any
blessing or help, we beg her to ask it from Jesus,
too."

" Does she hear all that way off ?"   asked
Charlie, gazing straight up above the chimney-
pots and roofs of the houses round.

" Yes ; quite as well as you hear me now.
She looks down upon us and loves us—she sees
you now, and wants you to be good and love her
dear Son Jesus Christ very much.   Now when

you look at this medal, will you think of the Blessed Virgin ?"

" Yes," said Charlie. " Is that all about it ?"

" No; not all. There are some words upon the medal which are a little prayer to the Blessed Virgin Mary. If you like to come with me into the school, I am going there now, and you will see the boys, and perhaps if I ask them some questions you will hear a little more about your medal. Does your mother want you ?"

" Not she," said Charlie. " She's glad to see the back of me."

So Father Bernard took the boy up into the school-room, where he was going to pay a visit before it closed for that day, and Charlie found a great number of eyes turned on him, as he followed the priest in at the door.

Many lads there knew him, and thought he was come as a scholar, but when Father Bernard kept him by his side as he went from one to another, or spoke to the schoolmaster, they wondered what Charlie Pearson did there. In a very few moments Father Bernard said he wanted to ask them a few questions.

" Now, boys, you have all medals of the Blessed Virgin on—or you ought to have. Are they any use to you ?"

"Yes, Father," shouted everyone in the room.

"Gently, gently. I'm not deaf.   Now tell me *how* they are of use ?"

No one answered, for no one knew exactly what to say.

"Come—does no one know ? Here, you— Pat Murphy, isn't it ?—tell me the use of your medal."

Pat looked suspiciously at Charlie—had he been telling of him, then ? if he had—but it was no time for thinking what he would do, with the priest waiting for an answer, and all the boys watching him, quite ready to laugh if he could not say.

"It's—it's—it's——" stammered Pat, getting very red.

"It's what ?" said Father Bernard, quickly.

"It's to remind us of the Blessed Virgin, Father."

"Yes; because we never think of her as much as we ought. We wear these little medals, so that seeing them and touching them may bring the Mother of Jesus to our minds. Now the figure upon the medal is that of Mary, is it not ? There are different kinds of figures of our Lady. Can any boy tell me what this particular one is

"The Immaculate Conception," shouted three or four.

" Quite right. And by that we mean that Mary was spotless and free from all stain of sin, even when she was conceived. Were any of us the same ?"

" No, Father," cried the boys.

" Were any of the saints free from all stain of sin ?"

" No, Father. Only Our Lady, because she was to be the Mother of Christ," said a very little boy at the end of one of the forms, close by Charlie Pearson.

" Now, boys, what are the words on your medals, which make a little prayer to the Blessed Virgin ?"

" O Mary, conceived without sin, pray for us who have recourse to thee," they answered all together.

" And that means that we ask our dear Lady, our sinless Mother, to pray for us who turn to her for help, does it not ?"

Again there was a universal shout of " yes."

" Supposing, boys, that some one was being tempted to commit a great sin. He is very near doing it, perhaps, only he does not quite like to be so wicked. If there was only a friend near to take him out of the way, he might be saved; but he hesitates and isn't quite brave enough to go from temptation by himself. If such an one suddenly thought of his medal—the medal of Mary who never sinned—would there be any help in it?

"Yes, Father; because then he'd be ashamed to do a sin," said Pat Murphy.

"I hope he would: he *ought* to," answered the priest. "But if, when he looked at it, he said that little prayer, it would be still better, would it not? Our Lady always helps us in any temptation and danger, if we ask her. So now, all of you, value your medals more than ever, and don't grieve your holy Mother by committing sin.

Father Bernard went away then, taking Charlie with him. "Now would you not like to be one of our school boys?" he asked. And Charlie said he thought he should.

"Do you understand any more about your medal?" said the priest.

"Y-e-s, a little," answered the boy. "I seem to see there's some use in it. I can't quite remember the words, but I think I can

make them out, now I have once heard them.
I can read a bit." So Charlie bade the priest
good-bye, and ran home to tell his mother all
that had been going on.

Mrs. Pearson was in a better frame of mind
by that time. She had got through most of
her work in Charlie's absence, and had half
forgotten the annoyance of the morning,
although she could not forget her husband,
or that he would probably return that night
much the worse for the company he had been
in. She didn't think she had done wrong in
taking Charlie to the priest. No; come
what would, she wanted him to grow up respectable, and not be his father over again;
and she knew that Father Bernard was very
good to the boys about there, and tried to
keep them out of harm. Yes, it was a good
thing she had made him a Catholic, and he
should be brought up in the Catholic school,
too; she would send him the very next day.
All this had been passing through Mrs. Pearson's mind during the time Charlie had been
away, so he could not have brought his news
at a better opportunity for being listened to,
and the result was that from the following

morning he became a regular scholar at St. Anne's boys' school.

Two years had gone by—the Pearsons were living in their old street, and old room, much in the same fashion we have seen, excepting that the husband had fallen deeper into bad habits, and so their misery and unhappines had increased. Charlie was nearly ten years old now, and had grown a tall strong boy, a good deal altered for the better, we must hope, through his constant attendance at the Catholic school. But now his mother came to the priest one morning with a long face. "I'm very sorry, Father," she said. "My boy's got on so well at the school, it's a shame to take him away, but his father says he's big enough to get to work, and I must find him some sort of a place."

"I am sorry for him to leave the school, Mrs. Pearson; he is still very young. What sort of place do you think you could get him?"

"Well, Father, he might go somewhere, and clean knives and boots, and do little odd jobs, I should say. Many a boy does at his age, and if he only got a shilling a week, it'd be something coming in. It's hard work to keep him, with his father spending half his wages in drink."

" It's very sad to see your husband going on as he does. It all comes from not having any religion, Mrs. Pearson. I wonder that you don't see that people who forget God, as you both do, are not likely to prosper."

Mrs. Pearson did not look pleased. She was quite ready to speak of her husband's " goings-on," as she called it, but she did not like to be classed with him.

" I'm sure there's no one can say anything against me," she began. " I work hard and try to keep the boy respectable——" But Father Bernard interrupted her.

" Yes, I believe all that. I see that you are steady and industrious, but still I must say, you forget God; you act as if there was no God, or heaven or hell."

"I don't know what I've done," said Mrs. Pearson, on the very verge of crying.

" Only that you never think of God, never pray to Him, never go to worship Him, never repent of your sins against Him. Is that 'doing nothing,' Mrs. Pearson ? Suppose you were to die suddenly what would become of your soul ?"

A more uncomfortable thought could not have been put before her. Mrs. Pearson hastened to speak of something else. "I hope, please God, I'll not die yet awhile, for my poor boy's sake. But I must be going, Father. I only wanted to thank you for all your kindness to him, and say I'm sorry to take him away from school ; but it's no fault of mine."

" I am very sorry, too. But I hope you will see that he comes regularly to Mass on Sundays ; and you should make up your mind to come with him, and see if things don't get easier for you then."

And so Mrs. Pearson went off, to think very uneasily all day of what the priest had said to her ; but she succeeded in putting the uncomfortable thoughts away, as she had done many a time before. Some day she really *would* think about being a Catholic, but not then : she would wait till she had more leisure !

Charlie Pearson was in place very soon, and " out " of it still sooner ; and for the next few

months he led a rather unsettled life, sometimes at work and sometimes not, and filling
up his spare time by games in the street
with companions who did him no good. He
was going back sadly all this while. When he
was at the school, and went regularly to his
confession, he had really tried to keep from
doing wrong; but now old bad habits returned, and again and again he fell into sin,
which did not seem to trouble his conscience
as once it would have done. Sometimes he
went to Mass, but it was not easy to do it
when there was no one to remind him—no
mother or father to say it was Sunday, and
start him off; while on the other hand there
were all the bad boys in the neighbourhood
to laugh him out of the idea, and persuade
him to amuse himself as they did. Now and
then Mrs. Pearson roused herself up to be
very angry with the boy, and drive him off to
church with threats and blows, but it was not
often she thought of it, and her own carelessness and bad example made her words useless
at all times. Again and again the priest went
after Charlie: once or twice he got him to
confession, and then it seemed that the boy

intended to begin afresh to lead a better life ;
but back in his home, amongst evil influences,
he forgot all his promises to Father Bernard,
and went on just as before.

One thing, and one only, Charlie was faithful in—the wearing of his little medal. Since
the day he had picked it up by the road-side
he had never parted with it, and sometimes—
though they were sadly few—he said the words
of that little prayer to the Blessed Virgin, and
a "Hail Mary" afterwards, as he had been
taught at St. Anne's school.

At such times Charlie always felt a great
wish to be a better boy—a great shame when
he thought of his life. If he had but let the
good Spirit work on his heart then, it would
have brought him back safely to the feet of
Jesus for pardon many a time ; but Charlie
put away the good resolution, and tried to
crush the sorrow which was rising—to forget
that Mary Immaculate was watching and
praying for him. But something was to happen
to bring him back to God again—pain and
danger and sickness which Charlie in good
health had never dreamed of.

Several ladies for whom Mrs. Pearson worked

helped her occasionally by presents of food and clothes for herself and her child, which were very acceptable to her; and it happened that just about this time Charlie was dressed in such a much more respectable jacket and waistcoat than usual, that even his father's notice was attracted by them on his return home one night.

He had been drinking hard that day—all his money was gone, and he looked round the wretched room to see if there, was nothing he could take and dispose of, to get more of the horrid spirit which was fast ruining his soul and body. Suddenly his eye lighted on Charlie, and with an oath he bade the boy give up his clothes—the old ones were good enough for him.

The boy hesitated—he was dreadfully afraid of his father, but he feared his mother too, and she was downstairs, talking to Mrs. Murphy. Whatever would she say or do, if he let his father take the jacket and waistcoat to get drink ? But Pearson was in no mood for waiting. Seizing the boy by the arm, he tore off the clothes ; but in doing so he dragged out the little medal bright no longer now, but still

the same, which he—half-tipsy though he was
—remembered well.

"Didn't I take it from you?" he roared.
"Didn't I say I'd have none of that sort of
thing?   Take that, and that," and heavy blows
fell upon poor frightened Charlie; but the
second stretched him on the floor, where he lay
as if dead, with the blood trickling from a
wound in his forehead, which he had struck
against the chimney-piece in falling.   When
Mrs. Pearson ran in, alarmed by the noise,
with most of the people in the house behind
her, she raised a scream of "Murder!" as she
saw Charlie; and lifting him in her arms
turned upon her husband, reproaching him with
killing his boy, and calling her neighbours to
fetch the police.

Pearson stood aghast—he was sobered now
—horrified at what he had done.   "Yes," he
said, slowly, "I've done it now; I've murdered
him.   Let 'em take me;" and he sat down
and wiped away the great drops of perspiration
which stood upon his forehead.

"No, no," said kind-hearted Mrs. Murphy,
pressing forward, "he's not dead.   See, he's
breathing; he's hurt and stunned by the fall,

but, please God, he'll live. Fetch a doctor some of you; and here, Mrs. Pearson, let's lay him on the bed."

Yes; Charlie still lived, but for many a day and night he was very near death—lying there unconscious of what had happened, and noticing none who came near; but his hot hand always grasped the little medal, and every now and then he murmured the words which were on it.

All this time the wretched father never left the boy's side. He would sit and watch him, in a half-stupefied way, and when Charlie stirred or groaned, he would groan too, and say, "May God forgive me. If he dies, I've killed him." Then he would glance at his wife, curiously, wondering why she never reproached him, but spoke to him, when she *did* speak, in a quiet tone he had not heard for years. He did not know how his misery and remorse were stirring up all the softer feelings in her heart, which cruelty had well-nigh crushed out of late; how she longed to make peace with him, there, by the side of their child, and promise to be a better wife than she had been!

Then came a night when the doctor said a

few hours would show whether the boy would live or die—when the father and mother watched him together, silently, sleeplessly. Again and again Charlie would start up and seize his little medal nervously, muttering, "He *shan't* have it, he shan't !" and then in broken words came the prayer, " O Mary !—O Mary !—conceived—conceived—without sin, pray for us ;" and then he would seem to sleep again. Or it would be scraps of the " Hail Mary, pray for us sinners now—and at the hour of our death."

Pearson listened in a perfect agony : at last he could bear it no longer. "Hour of our death !" he exclaimed. " He'll die, I know he will—he's a-talking about death, and it's a sure sign he's going. I can't bear it—I can't. I loved him—yes I did ; it's all this horrid drink that turned me into a brute. Oh, wife, I am sorry—sorry for it all ! I'm ready to do anything to make up for it. If only God lets the boy live, I promise here and now that I'll never be what I've been of late. I've learned a lesson I'll not easily forget."

Poor Mrs. Pearson !—she could only wipe her eyes and say, " I only hope you'll keep your word, John," and then look at Charlie again, wondering if morning would ever come, time went so slowly.

And so at last it was day, and Charlie Pearson slept—a peaceful quiet sleep; and the doctor came and looked at him, and went softly out again with a smile on his face, and a whisper that " he would do now." And rough John Pearson cried like a child with thankfulness, and his wife cried too ; and Mrs. Murphy laughed and cried together, and said many a " Hail Mary" as she went through her work that day, for she felt sure that the Blessed Virgin's prayers had saved the little lad's life.

During Charlie's illness, Father Bernard had come to the house frequently ; bending anxiously over the sick boy, hoping for some sign of consciousness, praying earnestly to God to spare him, if it was only for time to confess his sins, before his soul was called away ; and at these visits Pearson had behaved respectfully, as if all his old hatred of Catholic priests was forgotten in the trouble.

But on this day—when Charlie was almost out of danger, and still slept on so peacefully— as Father Bernard came to ask after him as usual, Pearson went forward and held out his great rough hand. "I'd be glad to shake hands with yer," he said, "if you're not above it. I've said hard things about yer, I've swore I'd do yer any harm I could, but you've done for me now. *I've* noticed yer coming here so kind and patient, just to see after my poor boy as I well-nigh killed, and I thank yer for it. I'll be made a Catholic now, or anything yer like, if it'll keep me from drink and bad ways. Shake hands again, sir, if you're not above it."

Above it !—a priest of Christ above anything which could show kindness to God's poor. Not he ! And Father Bernard shook the out-stretched hand as warmly as John Pearson could have desired, and uttered a fervent "God bless you !" and then Mrs. Pearson rushed down-stairs in a great state of excitement, to tell her friend Mrs. Murphy that her husband was "a-making up to the priest."

"Ah ! it's all happened beautifully," said the good woman. "Didn't I tell you it would come right by-and-by, that day, two years and more back, when you was in such trouble after you'd got Charlie christened ? I've great faith in those medals myself—they get a wonderful

lot of blessings for us. That's why I made the
boy go and find it, instead of taking the loss of
it so quiet-like. Well, Mrs. Pearson, it's good
news you've brought me this day. I never
thought to see the time when your husband 'd
make friends with the priest. God and His
Blessed Mother be thanked!"

There is little left to tell now about the Pearson family. Slowly but surely Charlie regained
health and strength once more—and he got
back health of soul as well as body; and after
humbly seeking pardon for his wanderings from
God, he began again to try and live as a
Catholic boy should do. He had many temptations to do wrong, many trials of his faith,
but then he had more to help him, for both his
father and mother had been baptized and received into the Church of Christ, and were trying to understand and do what it taught them.
And so it proved that Father Bernard was
right when he told Mrs Pearson that the neglect
of God was the root of all her misery. With
the wish to *know* what was right, and the effort
to *do* it, John Pearson gradually broke away
from the vice which had nearly mastered him,
and the friends who had drawn him on to sin.

He did not get free at once,—Oh, no ! It was a desperate struggle ; many times he was overcome, many more times he was ready to give up and say " there was no use in trying." But God kept him from this, and so at last he became one of the most respectable and sober workmen round about. Now that wages were not spent in drink, but were used for food and rent and clothing, home became comfortable again, and Mrs. Pearson worked away with a good heart to keep it so. And thus out of all the wretched past a better and happier life began for them ; and I think if either father, mother, or boy were asked what had worked so great a change for good, they would tell you the history I have told you now, of Charlie's medal.

CATHERINE'S PROMISE.

IT was four o'clock. The girls of S. Joseph's school came trooping out into the yard, talking, laughing, and disputing with each other as they went along the street in little groups of three or four, towards the part of the town where most of their homes were.

"I'm not coming after this week," said a tall girl, of perhaps thirteen years. "Mother says I've had schooling enough, and it's time I was doing something."

Those who were near gathered round to hear more, and Catherine Watson was delighted with the interest they took in her news.

"Yes," she added, "I'm going down in the country to live with mother's brother, and help take care of the children. It'll be a beginning, mother says, and by-and-by I can get to service."

Catherine's schoolfellows eyed her with great admiration. When one of them left it was mostly to go to some little place, and get about a shilling a week for nursing a baby or minding a shop. So this was a piece of good fortune, which was talked of amongst them more than anything else that night.

"Sister! Sister!" cried one of the first-comers next morning; "Catherine Watson's not coming after Friday." But Sister Agatha did not answer, for just that minute the clock struck and school had to begin. She waited until twelve o'clock, and then called the girl aside and asked her where she was going.

" I'm going to my uncle's a little way in the country, Sister. They want me to help take care of the little ones. He's mother's brother; but they're not Catholics, Sister."

Sister Agatha looked sorry. "Does your mother like you to go, Katie?" she asked. "Is there a chapel near, and will you be able to keep to your religion ?"

" Oh yes, Sister. Mother wouldn't let me go

else; and they've promised not to keep me
from my church."

"Well, Katie, I can only say I feel sorry.
Still if you keep very near to God, and pray to
Our Lady, you will be safe. I am only afraid
lest you should be careless, or trust to yourself,
and then you would surely fall."

Catherine did not say anything; in her own
heart she was thinking that "Sister" was
making rather a fuss without cause. Surely it
would be as easy to be a good Catholic in
Northwood as in London, she thought.

But the good nun knew better than Catherine
how great temptations might come from very
little things, and she prayed much for this girl
whom she had had under her care for several
years.

When the last day at school came, the children gathered round Catherine to say good-bye,
but her last words were with Sister Agatha.

"I'm going to Northwood on Monday, Sister,"
she said. "I'll go to the Holy Communion on
Sunday, and ask God to bless me."

The nun pressed the hand which was slipped
into hers. "Do so, dear Catherine," she said;
"and as long as you feel that you can do no-

thing by yourself, without God's help, you will be safe. Come into the chapel with me now, will you? and promise our dear Lord there that you will never be false to your faith."

Catherine went, and after kneeling before the altar in the quiet church for a few moments, she followed Sister Agatha out into the porch; and as she looked up into the kind face she knew so well, the nun saw that her eyes were full of tears.

"Now, Catherine, I shall not be afraid for you," she said. "If ever you are tempted to give up your faith, or to be careless about it in little things, I think God will make you remember the promise you have given Him to-day, when you knelt by my side."

Then they parted, Catherine to go home more thoughtfully than usual, the nun to her convent, praying as she went that Jesus and Mary would love and protect the child.

On the Monday morning Catherine Watson had left her mother, and early in the afternoon she was safely at her uncle's house, with all the little rosy, curly-haired children staring at her. My! what a number there were! all like small steps, one above the other—Annie, Sarah,

Bobbie, Jessie, and the rest of them. Catherine thought that first night she should never know one from the other, or any of their names ; but when they sat down to tea she counted the heads round the table, and found there were seven besides her aunt with the baby on her lap—so different to her own quiet home, where there was only herself and Joe, with their father and mother.

Before she began upon the thick slices of bread and butter her aunt had been cutting, Catherine made the sign of the cross. It was a habit her mother had been very strict about and Catherine did it that night as a matter of course ; but when she saw all the pairs of wide-open eyes looking, she flushed up hotly, and when her aunt burst out laughing it was worse still, and she felt ready to cry.

"Bless the child! you're just your mother over again," said Aunt Harriet. "It did always make me laugh to see all that crossing of herself. I'd most forgot the look of it ;" and she laughed again, and the elder of the children joined in so heartily that it ended in him choking over his bread and butter, which turned the subject. But Catherine

felt an uncomfortable remembrance rankling
in her mind all the evening. Certainly, it was
nothing *very* hard to bear—she had not been
scolded or interfered with, only laughed at,
but that was a new thing to Catherine,
and she thought the difficulties "Sister" had
warned her about were coming soon and
fast.

Next morning at breakfast, Catherine sum-
moned up her courage and made the sacred
sign again; she fancied no one had seen her,
but George's eyes were quicker than she gave
them credit for, and he pointed with his finger,
crying: "Father, father, look at her! She
did it last night, and this morning when
she got up, she was kneeling before a little
white figure and saying something and doing
that with her fingers again. Isn't it funny,
father ?"

The father looked across at Catherine but
he saw her face was flushed and her eyes wet
with tears; and instead of joining in the
general laugh he turned very angry, and
ordered George out of the room, much to his
mother's annoyance.

"Why can't you let the child be ?" she exclaimed. " He didn't mean any harm, and if folks make themselves ridiculous they must look out to be laughed at ."

" I've promised my sister that no one shall interfere with the girl. Her religion ain't the same as most of the folks here, but she's to be let alone in it. D'ye hear ?" said the man looking sternly round the table—upon which a sudden silence seized every one, his wife included; for John Lane was one whose word had to be obeyed.

What was the sudden thought which had flashed into his mind as he looked at Catherine; which fidgeted him all the way he walked to his work, and would not be driven away by whistling, smoking, or anything else ?

Only the memory of his childhood, when he and his sister (so much like Catherine was, too) went to the little Catholic church in their native village together, learned their catechism from the mother who had died so long ago, confessed their childish sins to, and received their First Communion from, the dear old grey-haired priest who had gone to his rest now. And since then ? Well, John Lane had gone away as a lad from home amongst those who had no religion, dropping first one thing and then another, until he only kept the name of Catholic after a time. But *that* went soon ! John had grown into a man to be counted a Protestant, to marry a Protestant wife, to forget almost the very name of his childhood's faith, until it all flashed back upon his mind as he glanced at his little niece Catherine. Certainly he had. no happy thoughts to keep him company that day.

Meanwhile Catherine was not much better off at home. Her aunt was out of temper because George—her pet, and eldest child— had been scolded, scolded too for his cousin's sake ; and so Mrs. Lane bustled about in a somewhat stormy way, making herself very unamiable without saying anything which could be spoken of.

"Come, child, don't stand about looking at me," she exclaimed to her young niece. "Hasn't your mother brought you up better than that ? You've come to set us all a pattern of goodness, haven't you ?—so make yourself busy."

Catherine winced under her aunt's sneer,

and asked rather timidly, "What she should do."

"Do? Why, wash the breakfast things and tidy-up, and nurse the baby—anything. Lor! there's no need to ask for something to do where there's seven children. You'll find that out before you're many days older."

Truly Catherine found it out before dinner-time came, for she had not a moment's peace; so surely as she thought she had rocked and cuddled the baby to sleep, it woke with a frantic squall the instant she laid it in the cradle; and there was her aunt calling to her to peel potatoes, and sweep rooms, and half a dozen other things.

"Sarah, you might as well rock baby asleep in the cradle," said Catherine, at last, to the biggest of the little girls. "I can't do anything while I have to nurse him."

Upon which Sarah replied, "Shan't!" and went to tell her mother that "Catherine wouldn't nurse baby any more."

In came Mrs. Lane, half-up to her elbows in soap-suds, which she was hastily rubbing off. "There! give him to me," she said, snatching the child hastily; "I wouldn't let any one do for my children if they've not a mind for it."

Catherine was half afraid, half angry; but she choked down her rising tears and said, "I only thought you wanted me to peel the potatoes, aunt, and I didn't know what to do with baby." But Mrs. Lane cut her short.

"There don't stand arguing, girl—it's the one thing I can't bear. Go and peel the potatoes, do! It's getting late, and your uncle will be home, and not a bit of dinner ready and nothing done. Ah me! if this is all the help I'm going to get, I wish you'd stopped with your mother in London, that I do with all my heart."

Catherine wished it too, most earnestly, and some bitter tears ran down her face into the pan with the potatoes. She thought of her mother, she thought of the school which she had fancied it such a fine thing to leave. What were the girls doing then? and Catherine glanced at the clock by the kitchen window; why it was just on the stroke of twelve! the bell would be ringing for the

Angelus. Well she would say it too—there at the sink, peeling potatoes—it didn't matter that she couldn't leave off, for Our Lady knew all about it, and knew that her aunt was watching her impatiently ; so Catherine repeated the familiar words, and felt better after them, and by the time her uncle came home and they sat down to dinner, all the angry feeling had gone from her heart, for she had resolved to try to be very patient even if her aunt was cross and unjust.

Just at that time though, Mrs. Lane was neither one nor the other; she had a quick temper but "didn't bear no malice," as she often said. When she saw Catherine conquer her feelings and turn to upon the potato-paring with a good will, she was really sorry she had been so sharp ; and made up for it by speaking extra kind at dinner, and seeing that the girl's plate was well filled. That never-resting baby had at last wearied itself out too and was asleep, so that the kitchen and every one in it was peaceful.

Several days had gone ; Northwood was not quite strange to Catherine Watson now ; she had learned to know all the names of the seven small cousins, and to distinguish Annie from Sarah and George from Bob. Her aunt found out that she had a very fair notion of household work, and was quick and willing, so things bid fair to run smooth—that is if one great difficulty could be got over.

Mrs. Lane had, like all of us, many weak points, but she owned to *one*, and was apt to say that "if she had a weak point it was to be stirring early in a morning." Hardly a "weak" point either—but a very strong one, in so far as it was good—yet one which Catherine did not share. She had always "been fond of her bed," as her mother phrased it, but her aunt had less gentle words for it, and it was the occasion of a great many sharp complaints on her side, and angry looks and thoughts from Catherine.

" It's as easy to get up one time as another," she would argue. " It's just the turning out that folks don't like, and it's as well done first as last;" but her niece did not think so, and stayed in bed for " just one more minute " until all the minutes were gone, and she had to hurry on her things and rush down to the kitchen, from which her aunt was calling to her to take the baby or wash and dress the children.

One thing Catherine never had left undone —her aunt might scold, the children call, the baby cry, but she knelt before her little image of Mary and said her morning prayers, whatever happened, and this was a good thing, but how much better if it had been done at the right time! How many scoldings she would have escaped, how many wandering thoughts prevented, as she hurried over the words; how much more help and grace gained from her prayers if she had given to them the minutes she gave to bed after she was called to rise in , the morning.

" You'd best speak to Catherine yourself," Mrs. Lane said one day to her husband at breakfast time, when she was specially vexed and cross ; " it's no use my saying a word. The baby might scream till it was black in the face, —bless it !—and she'd not come down, and I've begged her to get up, and called her, and nothing's any use."

Catherine turned very red and said nothing —her uncle, too, was silent, for he couldn't bear to be hard on her, she was so like her mother; so that Mrs. Lane talked on, complaining of the laziness and uselessness of all girls, but of this one in particular. "She's ever so long in kneeling before a white thing, mother," chimed in Annie. "Me and Sarah look at her, and she thinks we're asleep, and she kneels down and she says words—oh, ever so fast—and then she does that with her hand, you know," and Annie tried to imitate her.

"There—don't, child. I can't bear to see you aping those Catholic ways, even in fun. That's it, you see, John—that's the niece you have brought to be such a help to me—a saying her prayers to an image, when the children are all calling for their breakfasts, and this poor baby crying so as would melt any one's heart—if they had one. It's fine to be religious, isn't it?"

Catherine burst into tears—partly from vexation, but more from shame; *she* knew that her prayers were not the cause of her late appearance every morning; only her laziness was to blame.

"Indeed, uncle," she sobbed, turning to him, "I'm not more than a minute or two at my prayers; and I *must* say them, I promised mother, and our priest, and——"

"There, there, don't cry," interrupted her uncle; "your aunt don't mean to be angry, Katie; she's just as fond of you as can be, though she's a bit sharp now and then. No one's going to hinder you saying your prayers, but I should think you might get up a bit earlier, and there'd be no harm done. It's enough to vex your aunt, come now, isn't it, Catherine? —with all these seven children a-crying to be dressed, and you not up, fine bright mornings like this too?"—and Catherine was obliged to own she was wrong, and promise to do better.

She kept her word too, for that was the last time her aunt ever had reason to complain of her late rising, though sometimes in her own mind she lamented over the few minutes which her own children told her Catherine still gave " to the white image."

"It's only Catholics say prayers, is it, mother?" Sarah asked one day.

"Bless the child! no—everybody says prayers of course—or ought to, leastways."

"But we don't, mother," continued Sarah; "you haven't taught us any."

Mrs. Lane coloured, for Catherine was there. "Ain't you ashamed of speaking like that to your mother, you naughty child?" she said. "Don't I toil and slave for you from morning till night, and how am I to find time to be a-saying prayers like folks who have nothing else to do? We who work for our living ain't expected to say prayers except Sundays, and the parson does that for us in church."

Sarah said no more, and no one else spoke, but Catherine thought a good deal about it, Poor little untaught children!—wouldn't it be nice to teach them the "Hail Mary," now? But perhaps her aunt wouldn't like it; at any-rate she would wait a bit, for it wouldn't do to be in a hurry, and she hadn't been a week at Northwood yet. Still there could be no harm in telling them some of the tales Sister had told the school children, bits of the saints' lives, or old legends; and Catherine found it a capital way to get peace, for when she began they gathered round her with open eyes as well as mouths, in speechless surprise, "Good gracious me, girl!" her aunt would exclaim as she caught a word here and there in passing through the kitchen; "what's the good of cramming their heads with that outlandish stuff?" However, she didn't forbid it, so Catherine went on.

The Catholic hymns were more to Mrs. Lane's mind—the baby went to sleep when they where sung to him, and that was a blessing; and then the little children caught up the tunes, which sounded pretty in their clear shrill voices, even to those who were not as devoted to them as was their mother; but when one day she heard George and Bobbie shouting "I love the ˌPope!" in the front garden, she dragged them in and shook them vigorously. "Let alone that Catholic stuff, *do!* you naughty, wicked children," she said. "What d'ye think the clergyman will say if he hears you? He'd bring his stick to you, that he would, and make you go to school, too."

"School" was enough to frighten George and Bobbie; they instantly put their fists into their eyes, and said they "didn't want to go to school, they'd stop along with mother," upon which Mrs. Lane promised them they should, provided they never sang that "dreadful thing again."

Catherine expected to get into trouble about it, but she did not. Her uncle just said, in his quiet way, "I think, Katie, if I was you I'd drop that hymn about the Pope. I don't object to it myself; in fact—I—I shouldn't mention it to your aunt—but I rather like it. But it'd do a sight of harm about here, so I'll ask you just to keep to those sort of hymns that folks wouldn't notice so much. That one to the Blessed Sacrament, or some of them sort you know."

Catherine stared at her uncle in silent surprise. Wasn't he a Protestant, and how did he know anything about hymns to the Blessed Sacrament ?

" Do you like Catholic hymns, uncle ?" she asked.

" Yes," said Lane, and a strange look flitted across his face ; " that's to say, I like 'em and I don't like 'em. They remind me of too many things to be altogether pleasant."

" Do they sing them at the Catholic Chapel here, uncle ?" she asked, still wondering very much.

" I can't say, I never was inside," he replied. " It's a stiffish walk from here; you'll hardly manage it on Sundays."

" Oh, but I must, uncle. I can walk a long way. Besides, you see, I couldn't stop away; I shouldn't be a Catholic if I didn't go to Mass, and go to my duties."

" That'll rub off, most like," replied Lane. "Other folks besides you have meant to keep straight, and they haven't for all that. First one thing slips and then another, and before you know it you've got out of the way of everything, and then, you see, all goes wrong."

Certainly, "uncle" was talking strangely to-night.

" The priest told me to be very faithful, and he said if I asked God to keep me safe I could. And Sister Agatha talked to me so, and mother ——ah! I wouldn't forget my faith and disappoint them all, and besides there's my promise," and Catherine's voice sank into silence, for her thoughts had gone back to the church at home, and the moments she had knelt there by the dear nun's side in the half light which came in through the painted windows, promising Jesus in the Tabernacle to be true to Him and His Church.

Would it, indeed, be as her uncle said ? Would she let little duties pass by undone and so slip further and further from what was right ? No, no—*never* while she prayed to Our Lord and His Mother. Catherine was certain of it, and from her heart an earnest prayer went up to God there as she stood at the kitchen window by her uncle's side—a prayer which was broken in upon by her aunt's shrill cry, " Catherine ! Catherine ! come and put the children to bed."

Next day was Sunday. Ah ! what a long week it had seemed since Catherine left London, but first weeks in a strange place are always so to every one. Yes, at last it was Sunday, and she got up in good time, with a lighter heart than usual, because she felt it would be so happy to be amongst Catholics for a little while.

John Lane had told her there was Mass at half-past ten—that would be a good time for her aunt to spare her, only she must allow more than half an hour for the walk, for the chapel was a longish distance from North-wood.

Catherine had to step about briskly certainly that morning; never did the children appear so tiresome, never did her aunt require so much help; never, surely, did the baby seem so determined not only to be nursed, but to be nursed by Catherine. If it hadn't been that her uncle took pity on her and ordered her to start, she would never have got off at all. As it was, Mrs. Lane grumbled at the girl going. "*She* never got time for church going—not she. Nobody cared though, oh, no. She might toil and slave six days in the week, and no rest on Sundays either."

"Come now, clap on your bonnet, and take the young 'uns, and be off'," cried her husband; "I didn't know you were so fond of church. I'll mind Jessie and the baby for you."

"Lor, John!" cried his wife, "you must be off your head. When did you see me a-dressing myself up and going to church? I leave that sort of thing for them as like it. It don't seem to me as the parson's much the better for his prayers; he don't do half the good to his poor people as the priest does, for all he's a Catholic, and one can't expect so much of him."

Lane laughed. "I'm glad you think the priest the best of the two. You'd better go along and hear his prayers with Catherine next Sunday."

"Heaven forbid!" cried Mrs. Lane, piously; "I wouldn't set my foot inside a Catholic church for any money; a pretty example for the children!"

"You're hard to please," said John. "Just now you were a-wanting to go to church, and next it seems neither one sort or the other 'll suit you. You'll have to stay at home, I'm afraid. Well, it comes to one thing, it'll be all the same in a hundred years," and he whistled and went to lean on the garden gate, and glance along the road Catherine had taken, and think he should uncommonly like to take a look at that church up there; it was many long years since he'd been inside one—perhaps he'd go one of these Sundays—anyway, he'd go and meet the girl.

He did so, and Catherine reminded him more than ever of her mother at the same age, as he saw her coming in the distance dressed so neatly in her Sunday clothes, looking brighter and happier than she had done before.

"You're all the better for going, Katie," he said kindly, taking her little prayer-book from her hand—" Garden of the Soul! Lor! I remember it perfectly; times enough I've carried a book like this when I was no bigger than Georgie. I'll take a look in at your Catholic place one of these days, Katie "—a promise which made Catherine very glad, although it was not carried out for many a week.

We must suppose now that several months have gone. Summer and autumn are over, winter is just beginning, and Catherine Watson is still at Northwood, getting so useful and handy that even her aunt owns she "couldn't do without her."

Friends at home do not forget the child— her mother writes to her often, prays for her oftener; the priest inquires for her whenever he visits her parents; Sister Agatha remembers Catherine and her promise, asks God to watch over her and guide her all her life.

And is Catherine faithful still? Has she forgotten her early training? Does she prize her religion less or grow careless in practising it ?

Well, Catherine has found out that Sister Agatha was right when she warned her of difficulties. There have been times when she has felt it hard to do right; tiresome to plod along muddy lanes or through driving wind and rain to weekly Mass; vexing to sit down to a nice dinner on Friday, which she must not eat, but be content with the bread and butter the others laugh at. The months which have gone have brought many a fall, many a broken resolve, but by God's grace they have brought many an act of contrition, many a prayer for pardon; they have taken her to the Sacraments for grace to make fresh beginnings, and so Catherine is faithful to her promise—she is striving through all those failings to be a true child of the Holy Church.

The sharp frosty air suited the little hardy children in John Lane's cottage, and made their red cheeks firmer and rosier than ever, and brought a colour and freshness to Catherine's face which she never had in London.

But Mrs. Lane had taken cold—a cold which clung to her in a way the active, healthy woman

" had no patience with," as she said! and yet in spite of all her efforts she was forced to give in at last, and leave the house and children on Catherine's hands for a while.

How hard it was for Catherine every one could see. How hard it was to be patient and gentle, and bear with her aunt's irritable temper, and the children's trying ways, no one but herself knew—except God and her good Angel, who helped her to do right.

But days went by and Mrs. Lane grew worse; until even she, who had always scorned the idea of illness, began to fidget about herself.

" It'd be a bad thing if anything happened to me; I don't know what John and the children would do. You'd stay, Catherine ?" she said, one evening when the little ones were asleep and they two were alone together.

All Mrs. Lane's scoldings and tempers were forgotten, then. Catherine felt a real love to her aunt as she kissed her and said, " Oh don't talk so! I'd stay and do anything, but you'll get better."

" Perhaps so, perhaps not !" was the answer. " I've been thinking a deal about it, Catherine, a-wishing I'd my time over again. There's many things I'd do different. I wonder if I'd feel more easy like, now, if I'd kept to church-going, like some folks ?"

Catherine hardly knew what to say. "Would you like to see your clergyman, aunt ? Wouldn't he help you to feel easier ?"

" Bless you ! no, child. He's been no good to me all my life, 'tisn't likely he'd be any use now I'm bad.   Besides, he'd not trouble himself to come so far unless it was convenient. I think I'd as soon you said some of your prayers for me, Katie; they'd do as much as his talking, any way."

" I do pray, aunt. I've asked Our Lady every day that you may get better."

" You'd best pray to God, child ; He can do it without any one to help."

" Yes, but if Our Lady asks too, it helps us get what we want, you see, aunt ?"

" No, I don't see," said the sick woman. " I feel bad to-night, and can't stand much talking.   Dear ! dear ! if anything happens to me it'd be dreadful for John and the children. My head seems to run wild like, and that's a bad sign. I keep thinking over old times, when I was a little thing at home with my mother. Ah! she *was* good. Somehow I never took after her, but I remember lots of things she used to teach me now; it seems coming back to me to-night."

The room was quiet for a while after that, and Catherine thought her aunt slept; so she knelt down by the bedside and began to say her rosary, but she had not gone through the second mystery before Mrs. Lane's eyes opened again.

"I wish John would come home, he'd be some comfort;" but almost before she had ceased speaking his step was on the stairs, and Catherine ran to meet him, and then went to see to the baby and other things which were wanted.

It seemed a long, long night, but at last it was over, and Catherine hurried to her aunt to see how she was, the first thing.

"She's awful bad, Katie," said her uncle. "One time she's sensible like, and another she don't remember anything, but keeps talking about her mother and things which happened years back. The doctor's been, and he says it's a feverish cold that's caught hold of her. She seems to think a deal about dying, and she isn't happy in her mind—that's what bothers me."

Catherine could not help wishing she was in a Catholic house, she would know what to do then ; however, she went into the room silently and looked at her aunt. " I'm no better, Catherine ; seems to me I get worse. I wonder if I'd best send for the parson ? Lots of people do when they're feeling as bad as me, but I can't see the use of it. It isn't a lot of talking I want, it's some one as can *do* something."

" If you were only a Catholic," faltered Catherine. " Oh ! aunt, don't be vexed with me. If you were, you know, I'd fetch the priest, and he *could* do something — he could forgive you your sins."

" Ah ! that would be worth a good deal," murmured the woman. " I haven't led a bad sort of life, I've done my duty to John and the children, and I've been as good as my neighbours, and yet there's all manner of things trouble me. I don't know how it is I've forgotten so long, but now I keep thinking what mother used to say, that when I died I'd have to stand before God. I am *afraid*, Catherine, that's what's worrying me now and making me worse than I should be. I'm not ready to die, and I don't see as the parson's talking would make me so."

"No, aunt, I don't see that it would. But if the priest came that's so different, because he could give you God's pardon."

"I wish I believed he could; I'd send for him right away. But somehow I don't see how he can. I——" But John Lane had come into the room, and he stopped her there by turning round on Catherine with a sharpness that was strange to him.

"Don't waste the time a-talking," he said; "run, like a good girl, and fetch the priest. It'll be a deal better than arguing about it. Never mind whether she don't see the good of him; she'll *feel* it the first moment he sets foot in the room. Don't I know enough to be sure of that?"

Catherine needed no second bidding. She just waited to cut the children a thick slice of bread each to bribe them to stay quietly in bed till she came home, and then she started, first running and then walking, and then running again, along the road.

It was very cold, the sky was thick and yellow,

and little short gusts of wind came whistling past her every minute as she hurried on; then a single flake of snow came down, and then another, and another, until, before Catherine reached the priest's house, the road before and behind, and the paths on each side of it, were completely covered. In her hurry and excitement the snow seemed pleasant enough at first, but she felt so benumbed with the cold, that just as she got to the end of her journey she was not far from crying; but the kind words of the priest set her right at once. He would come to her aunt—come almost directly, he said; and Catherine started home as quickly as she could, leaving Father Kelly to follow.

Her uncle met her at the door. "Is he coming?" he asked, and at Catherine's nod his face brightened. "I've a deal of faith in priests," he said. "I've heard of times when the mere look of 'em was worth more than a dozen bottles of doctors' stuff," and he went back to his sick wife, feeling much relieved.

Catherine was busy with the children, but she was thinking of her uncle. Really he talked about Catholics as if he believed in them. Surely he could easily be taught to know more.

Ah, wouldn't it be pleasant if he turned one himself! and the children too, and her aunt! But here Catherine's happy fancies were stopped by the priest's knock at the cottage door.

As soon as Father Kelly was inside the sick room, John Lane bolted off to his day's work. There were reasons, which no one but himself knew, which made him fight shy of a priest, and reasons too which made him start with a light heart and a firm belief that "the missis" would be better when he went home at noon; for, through all his faithlessness and falseness, John had never believed in any other religion. He had tried to do without it, but he had only found out since Catherine came that the old reverence of his boyhood for the Catholic Church was still in his heart—very far down, very much over-grown by carelessness and sins, but not wholly lost. All that morning, as he sawed and planed and hammered, he was having a sharp time of it; for his conscience would not be hushed to sleep any longer. He was thinking how different things might have been — *ought* to have been; but happily there was time still. By God's grace this illness of his wife might be a chance for him, and for them all to get right at last.   That was how he comforted himself.

"What's the news ?" said John, as Georgie and Annie and Sarah rushed to meet him before he opened the garden gate.

"Mother's better ! mother's better !" they shrieked.

"Yes, uncle; she seemed very quiet and calm after Father Kelly went away, and then she fell asleep ; and the doctor's been, and he said it had done her good, and that he thought she'd mend now," added Catherine.

"I told you a priest was worth more than the doctor," said John.   Then, meeting her surprised look he added, "I've heard my mother say it when I was a youngster, Catherine."

Truly Mrs. Lane seemed better; the worrying and restlessness were gone, and she slept quietly at intervals through the rest of the day and night ; and before long she was well enough to talk to John of what had happened.

"Only to think how I've spoke against Catholics !" she said.   "And, now all I care about is to learn to be one of them.   Ah ! that *is* a good man, that Father Kelly, John ; it made me feel better directly he came and sat down so quiet

like and began talking, and after a bit I got
a-telling him everything that troubled me—
same as if I'd known him all my life. You
won't mind, John, will you? He's coming to see
me again. You never said anything against
Catholics. Your sister's one, and Catherine
here, and she's a good girl, if ever there was
one."

But John answered not a word, but went out
of the room so suddenly that his wife concluded
he was angry about it, and yet she hardly knew
why. Certainly the priest's coming was John's
own doing after all, as she said to Catherine.

At the end of a week Mrs. Lane was so nearly
well that the doctor had ceased to visit her, and
so much quieter and kinder and more thoughtful
that any one might have been surprised at the
change, unless they had believed in the power
of Father Kelly's visits and words as fully as
Catherine did. The only thing that was trou-
bling the poor woman was whether John was
vexed about her " turning to the Catholics," as
she called it ; and she wondered how she could
best make it right with him.

One evening they were talking together, and

she said, " I've a deal to ask you to forgive,
John.   I've let my temper be a trouble to you,
and I've not been as good a wife as you deserve ;
but please God I'll do better now."

" Don't !" cried John; "don't go on like that,
I can't stand it.   It's I who've got to be forgiven.   I've deceived you and every one ; I'm a
Catholic—yes, that I am—though a false, bad
one.   I was brought up as much a Catholic as
my sister, and though I've forgot it, and been
ashamed of it, and denied it for many a year, I'll
out with it now to all Northwood, and we'll
start fresh—you and me together, wife."

What a surprise it was, and what a pleasure to Catherine—a happiness she had never
dreamed of — when her uncle called her to him
and said, " God bless you, girl ! He sent you
here to wake us up, to make me ashamed of
myself.   Every time I looked at you trudging
off to Mass, and keeping so straight in everything, it regularly cut me to the heart— that it
did.   It was a happy day for all of us when
you came here, and now you may write and tell
your mother.   She's been a-wishing and praying for this, many's the year."

Was Catherine satisfied and pleased with herself? Ah no! Conscience told her of too many faults and failings for her to let pride come in; but she did thank God very heartily and humbly that He had helped her to keep her promise, and made her of use for His glory.

There was nothing else talked of in Northwood for some days when it was known that John Lane, his wife, and the seven children, were all "turned Catholics." The parson himself came as far as the door to talk with Mrs. Lane; but it was to no purpose, so he left her with the warning that she was leading her children to destruction. "No, sir, begging your pardon," she answered; "we've set our faces right the other way, since we've been Catholics;" and so they parted.

After a little while the affair was forgotten. George and Bobby might shout "I love the Pope!" to their hearts' content now, and nobody hindered them; and so they settled down into a new way of things—a better and happier way than had ever been before.

The good news had been sent up to Catherine's mother in London, and she had told the priest and the Sister at St. Joseph's school what her brother had written about Catherine, and how he said they could not possibly spare her to come home for a long time.

But Catherine sent a little note of her own to Sister Agatha.   It took a great many evenings writing on the kitchen-table, for accidents were always happening — either George jogged her elbow, or the baby pulled the ink-bottle over, or something of the same kind—so that three or four beginnings were made before a letter was finished, and sealed, and dropped into North-wood post-office.   It was not very long, but it told the nun that Catherine had often done wrong, had often been half-tired of her faith, but the memory of the few minutes spent in St. Joseph's church, that last day of school, had kept her from giving up ; and it ended by say-ing, " And uncle's a Catholic, and so is aunt, and all the children, and we are so happy.   They say it's all through me, Sister, but *I* think it's through you, and God told you how to help me."

Sister Agatha was out when that letter reached the convent ; she came home one wet cold afternoon, very weary, very sad, for the school-children had grieved her that day by behaving unusually ill.   But when the care-fully-written note was given to her, she was so

glad, that she thought no more of being tried,
and all her sadness went away as she knelt
before her Lord in the little convent-chapel,
and thanked Him for helping Catherine to be
true to her promise.

NORAH'S TEMPTATION.

CROWDS of people were hurrying along the street, all going somewhere; but every one was taken up with his own business and did not even notice poor Norah Brian, who was feeling almost as lonely as if she was the only person in the world.

It was getting late; there was a cold, raw fog, and the girl's teeth chattered, for her clothes were thin and poor.   She looked at the faces of all the passers-by with a sort of hope that she might see some one to speak to, some one to tell what distress she was in; but one after another passed on, and Norah was losing courage, and dared not follow them.

She had been up and at Farringdon Market before five o'clock that morning, to buy water-cresses, and then she had to wash them and tie them up in bunches ready to sell, before she could begin her weary rounds, and cry "Water-*creases*, three bunches a penny, water-*creases.*" People knew her voice well enough, but had seldom thought of Norah. Sometimes she had plenty of customers and sometimes not, but on this particular day she had not been fortunate; and as it seemed no use standing in the streets any longer, she wrapped her ragged shawl about her and prepared to move on. Just then, a lady who was passing hailed a cab from the stand near by, and as Norah watched her get in and direct the driver where to go to, her sharp eyes noticed something bright and glittering drop on the pavement. She sprang forward and picking it up, held it under her shawl until the cab had driven away.

Then Norah peeped at her prize very cautiously, first glancing round to make sure no one saw her. Ah! what a lucky day for her! —it was a bracelet, worth ever so much money, the girl felt sure—money which would help mother and the little half-starved children at home. That was the first thought; the next was very different. Some voice in Norah's heart said that the bracelet was not hers, that to keep it would be dishonest, more than that, it said that she had been wrong in letting the owner of it drive away unconscious of her loss, that she had been guilty, in thought, of stealing—troublesome whispers of conscience which were very difficult to turn a deaf ear to.

Then Norah tried to think that she was doing no harm ; she had *found* the bracelet, and the lady who had lost it was gone, and she should never see her again ; surely there could be no harm in selling it to get firing and food and clothes for father, who was ill, and mother and the children, who looked so pale and wretched ?

All this time Norah Brian was trudging along to Spencer's-court, where she then lived. Rude dirty children were all about, and idle, quarrelsome men and women, but she was quite used to the sights and sounds which were there, and passed through them all without taking much notice of any one, thinking only of the glittering bracelet in her pocket, as she went up the crooked, narrow stairs, to their room at the top.

What a place it was ! The poor sickly father lay on some rags which once had been blankets, in one corner, whilst in another, near the broken window was Norah's mother, working hard in the failing light at some shoe-binding she did for a shop in the city. A baby was asleep in an old basket, and three more rough-headed children were playing on the floor with some empty reels and oyster-shells, and other rubbish they had brought in from the street.

Mrs. Brian looked up at Norah's half-empty basket. *That* told her it had not been a good day ; and as the girl gave her the money she had earned, the poor woman sighed heavily. She had reckoned on being able to get out for a little tea and bread for their supper that night, but they must go without, for the rent had been falling behindhand several weeks, and the little Norah brought must be put by towards that, or they would be turned out of even that miserable shelter.

" Well, if things don't mend, there's nothing but the workhouse before us," she said. " I toil and slave day after day, and far into the night, and yet it's hard to keep body and soul together."

" Why don't some one help us, I'd like to

know ?" murmured the sick man. " There's folks as don't know what to do with their money, they've got so much; and we may starve. It's hard lines, that it is ; it's enough to drive us poor to take what's not ours."

" God forbid !" exclaimed the wife. " We're poor, Heaven knows, and well-nigh starving sometimes ; but I'd rather die outright than have any one of mine take what wasn't theirs. We're not *that* sort."

Brian went on grumbling to himself. Poor fellow ! it *was* " hard lines," as he would say, to lie there useless, when medicine and food would have set him up again, and made him able to seek for work. Fourteen weeks he had been doing nothing, for a fall from a ladder had lamed him and then he had grown weak and low, and seemed almost wasting away ; while his wife with her shoe-binding, and Norah with her watercresses, were trying to support the family. It was little help they got, either. The priest who visited Brian did all that was possible, but his means of assisting them were very small; and there were many Catholics living in the courts and alleys in that crowded part who were even in greater distress; and all these were looking to him for what he could not give—money, food, clothes.

That night, when Norah lay down on the old rug which was her bed, she felt every now and then at her pocket where the bracelet was hidden, to see if it was still safe; and then she began planning how and where she could sell it, and above all how she could keep her secret from her mother, for Norah dared not tell her what had happened. She knew quite well that no hunger or distress would tempt Mrs. Brian to keep money so obtained, and that if she knew of the bracelet, her first act would be to take it round to the priest's house, and ask him what was to be done about it. So, after all, the "luck" did not make Norah as happy or comfortable as she had thought when she walked off with the prize she had found. She dared not sell it, for she feared that at any shop she might go to they would suspect her —a dirty, ragged little water-cress-girl — of not having come by it honestly. She dared not hide it at home, for, indeed, there was no hole or corner where she could be sure it would not be found by the prying eyes of the younger children. There was nothing for it but to carry the bracelet pinned up in her pocket as she went to market, and sat on doorsteps, and walked the streets, crying " Water-*creases* ;" and many a time Norah wished that she had never seen it, never had the disagreeable secret in her mind, which bothered her by day and night. Somehow Norah felt a strange fear when a policeman passed her ; it would have seemed as if she expected him to see into her pocket, and finding the gold bracelet there, pounce upon it and carry her off for stealing.   She slunk along now, and dodged round corners, and hid behind walls, as if she was the veriest little thief in London.   Now and then she would wish she should happen to meet with the lady who had lost the bracelet.   Norah felt sure she should know her again, for she had stared at her well— at her face and nice clothes — and could have recognised her anywhere, even though she had only seen her an instant in the dusky light. But then it would be very awkward to explain why she hadn't given it up at once.   Perhaps, however, she might get out of that difficulty by saying the cab had driven off too quickly, or some other story ; and then the lady would give her a reward for being honest, and she could take it home and tell the tale to her mother, and there would be supper and warmth and comfort, at any rate for a little while. That was one ending to her difficulty, which Norah's fancy conjured up ; but it so happened that this day-dream never came true—not the least bit of it, excepting that she did see the lady again, in the very last place where she should have thought to look for her.

It had been Monday when Norah went home with her secret; now it was Sunday, and her mother was trying to get them all a little cleaner and neater for Mass. The bell of the church was ringing loudly, a few Catholics were hurrying that way, but unfortunately, many more were lying sleepily in bed, or idling in the doorways; and, for once, Norah would have liked to be amongst the number who forgot or disregarded that it was Sunday and church-time.

It was only a " wish." There wasn't one of the little Brians who would have dared to speak of such a thing as missing Mass without cause.

Through all her poverty and troubles their mother had kept strictly to the habits she had

been trained in as a child in her Irish home;
and, with shoes or without, cold or warm,
hungry or not hungry, she and Norah, with the
two next in age, were always down on their
knees at the door of their parish church during the Holy Mass, whilst the baby and the
next youngest were left at home to amuse
themselves as best they could with the reels,
and oyster-shells, and other things, which we
have already seen were their only toys.

It was very little Norah knew of reading, so
a book would have been useless to her; but
she always carried her red rosary to church on
Sunday—the one which had been give her at
her First Communion.

On that particular day Norah couldn't say
her beads, couldn't pray—I was going to say
could not *think;* but, indeed, she was doing
nothing else but think all through Mass, only
it was about that bracelet which she still
carried, which she put her hand on every time
any one pressed against her in the crowd, to
make sure it was there still. Oh, dear! there
were Mary and Katie O'Leary with new hats
on, and Maggie Sullivan, had a pair of boots.
Here Norah looked down at her feet, which

came peeping out at the sides of the old shoes she wore, which were ever so many sizes too big for her, and went "slip-slopping" up and down as she walked. Now, if she could only get some money for the bracelet, she'd have a pair of boots, and a new hat and a frock too! —yes, that she would, and so should Polly and Janie! So Norah's eyes wandered round the church, and her thoughts wandered worse—none were given to God, none to the holy adorable Sacrifice which was being offered up—none to the Mother of Christ, or the blessed saints in heaven, and the little red rosary had been small use to her when all was over, the people leaving their places, and she with her mother and Polly were making their way through the crowd at the door.

"Bless us and save us, child! What's the matter?" cried Mrs. Brian, as Norah suddenly darted aside, and almost hid herself in her mother's shawl. There was nothing to be seen — only ladies, gentlemen, children — old, young, rich and poor, pouring out of the big church and going homewards; yet Norah seemed frightened and could not give any reason for it either which satisfied her mother.

The fact was, she had caught sight of the well remembered face of the lady whose bracelet she carried in her pocket, and with an instinctive consciousness of guilt she had tried to hide herself. But there was no need for it; the owner of the bracelet had never caught a glimpse of Norah that Monday evening when she watched the cab drive off, and hurried to secure the prize; if she had, I doubt if she would have recognised the dirty little face and and figure amongst the crowd who were coming out of the church; it was Norah's conscience which frightened her, and kept her so silent all the rest of the day.

The lady was a Catholic then. Perhaps she always came to that church, and Norah would see her sometimes. Ah, then it wouldn't be so very hard one day to go up to her and say : " Please, ma'am, is this yours ?" and get paid for giving up the bracelet. Yet it happened that on several Sundays following this chance came, and somehow Norah was seized with a sudden terror and trembling, and dared not do it. Besides, she thought her mother would sure to look round and miss her, and turn back when she saw her speaking to a lady. Ah ! it was an awkward piece of business altogether, and Norah resolved that it should be the last time she would ever meddle with what was not her own.

Christmas time was coming very near then, and a fresh difficulty was before Norah. How about going to confession ? Well, she wouldn't, that was all; she'd say she didn't want to go, and her mother would be angry, of course, but it was no use minding; she couldn't hide what she had been doing if she went to the priest, and now, after all this time, she was afraid to own her sin. But this resolution did not make Norah Brian happy; she hadn't missed her Christmas Communion since she had been old enough to make it, and Father Russell would come and see after her, and she shouldn't know what to say when he spoke to her of the Holy Child whose feast she had neglected, just as she could guess he *would* speak.

All this while Norah was going on with her work as usual, only she had taken to selling oranges in the afternoons, now that it was Christmas time, and school-boys were likely to be customers, and gentlemen might buy them for home. On the whole she did pretty well, and yet her earnings were nothing near enough to help her mother as she wanted to. In three days the 25th of December would be here, and the shops were full of good things, and people looked happy, and hurried along with parcels and packages, and the whole city seemed full of rejoicing, except in poor homes like the Brians', and many others in the narrow streets and turnings which were forgotten or unknown by those who were rich and happy.

" We're going to have a pudding," a child had said, who lived in the same house, up Spencer's-court; and then Norah had grown desperate. Yes, she would risk the danger of being suspected, she would walk a long way to some distant shop, and get rid of that bracelet which still weighed down her pocket, and weighed more heavily on her heart. She must make up some tale to tell her mother as to the way she came by the money, and they would have a pudding too, and meat perhaps, and keep Christmas merrily for once.

" Wrong ? Well, it wasn't worse than what

she was doing now; she had kept the bracelet all this time, when she could have given it back over and over again. Yes, she was really a thief now, and it wouldn't be any worse to sell it, and get something good out of it at last." That was what she tried to believe, but yet that awkward voice of conscience tried to be heard once more, and reminded her that even now, after all the past, she could get peace, and pardon, and help by going to confess the truth to God, and obeying the directions of the priest who was His messenger.

There was a great struggle in the girl's heart, but the bad angel got the best of it then; and without any more delay Norah Brian trudged on to a distant part of the town, and entered a smart looking jeweller's shop, unpinned her pocket, took the bracelet, and with a hand that she tried hard to keep steady, held it out to the man behind the counter and asked him to buy it.

A strange figure Norah looked in that shop, so full of rich things, so warm and well lighted. She was dirty, ragged, and mud-stained, her basket of oranges still on her arm—but n early empty now, for she had had a good day—and her face was flushed partly from nervousness and partly from the haste she had been making.

There were several customers in the shop, who turned and stared at the girl—just as the jeweller stared at her, while he held the bracelet in his hand and twisted it round and about suspiciously for a few seconds—seconds which seemed hours of torture to Norah. At last he spoke out sharply and quickly : " How did you come by it—stole it, didn't you ?"

" Oh, no sir ! Please sir," said Norah, in a desperate fright, " I picked it up one night, four or five weeks ago, and I've kept it on purpose to give it back. But I can't find who it belongs to, sir ; and father's bad and out of work, and there's four of us at home, well-nigh starving ; and mother said I'd best try and get a trifle for it to-night, as it's fairly ours now, so as to buy us something for Christmas."

" A very likely tale," said the jeweller ; "I've heard it before, often. I don't believe a word, of it, either. I think the best thing I can do is to hand you over to a policeman."

Poor Norah ! Was that to be the end of all her planning, all the falsehoods she had made up to tell, of all her hopes of a Christmas pudding ? She thought of home and her mother, and glancing timidly around, she darted to the open door; but the jeweller was quicker, and now feeling sure of her guilt, did not hesitate to hold her fast until a policeman was brought.

"Perhaps she told the truth. You've frightened her," said a kind old gentleman, who had been looking on in silence. "Wait a bit, Mr. Johnson ; let me speak to the child. Now, my girl, don't be frightened, no one shall hurt you. Tell me your name and where you live."

" I'm Norah Brian, please, sir, and I live up Spencer's-court; and oh, please, don't have me took by the police !"

" No; I don't mean to," said the old man ; " that is, unless I think you deserve it. Now, is that the truth you've told Mr. Johnson ?"

Norah looked up into the kind old face which was bent towards her. She would have told the real true tale to that gentleman, if she had not been there in the shop, with the sharp-eyed jeweller listening, and his boy standing ready to fetch the policeman. As it was, she burst into tears and said—

"Yes; I found it weeks ago, in the streets where I was a-selling my water-creases; and we're so poor, and I've had nothing to eat scarcely to-day, and it's Christmas, and I wanted to get some dinner for mother and the little ones."

The old man turned to the jeweller. "I will see to the matter. You need do nothing more. I shall find out the truth of the tale. Now, my little girl, will you show me the way to your home? We will leave the bracelet with Mr. Johnson for the present."

Norah was desperately frightened, and yet anything was better than the dreaded policeman. So she took up her orange-basket and led the way to Spencer's-court, wondering very much what the end would be, and what her father and mother would say.

On they went, through dark passages, round corners, across crowded streets, until they had reached Spencer's-court, and there Norah led the way to her mother's room, with the old gentleman close behind her. On the way, he had asked her so many questions, that he was quite sure it would be a poor place which he was taken to, but he had not expected such great misery as he saw, when Norah opened the door. No fire, the sick father in his corner, the pale, wan mother bending over her work, and the little children, who just then were crying for food.

When Mrs. Brian saw the kind-looking old gentleman who came in with Norah, she thought it was in answer to her prayers that God had sent a friend to help them. She was not prepared to hear such a cause for his visit as that which he began to tell, whilst Norah hung down her head and cried so bitterly.

"Bracelet, sir?" repeated Mrs. Brian. "I don't understand. Norah hasn't found anything that I know of."

"Then they were all falsehoods you told, were they?" said the old man, turning upon Norah, with a look of disappointment on his kind face. "I might as well have let the policeman take you then, but I believed you were telling the truth when you said your mother sent you."

"Police? Take Norah?" cried the mother. "Oh, sir, there's some mistake, for though we're poor we're honest, and there isn't a child of mine 'd lay hands on anything, I do believe. Norah, what is it? Look at your father. You're making him worse; you'll kill him! What have you been doing, child?"

Norah looked piteously at the old gentleman.

"Oh, sir, I'll tell the truth now; it wasn't *all* lies I told in the shop. I did find the bracelet, but I made up about mother sending me to sell it." And after a great deal of questioning, the whole history came out, and Norah, sobbing bitterly, declared "that was all, quite all," and once more begged their visitor not to give her up to the police.

"And you never told me, Norah!" said her mother. "And you could see the lady again and again, and not give her her bracelet! I couldn't have believed it, if I hadn't heard it from your own mouth. Dear, dear! that I should live to find a child of mine no better than a thief!"

Brian had half-risen up with the excitement of the scene, and now he spoke. "Let her go, wife," he cried; "let her be locked up, if they like. *I'll* not screen her. I'll not have it thrown in my face that a girl of mine acted so. Get out of my sight, Norah, and——" but the gentleman checked him angrily.

"Shame on you, man!" he said, "turning against your own child like that. She's done wrong, very wrong, but if she's sorry—and I believe she is—God will forgive her."

"I'm not a-going to be disgraced by the girl," repeated Brian; but he lay down again, and the effort had exhausted him so much that he said no more. It was not the sin which troubled Brian, for he was not, like his wife, a good Catholic: it was the disgrace which he felt from Norah's dishonesty coming to light.

"So you are a Catholic," said the gentleman, turning to Mrs. Brian. "The lady who owns this bracelet is one, too, I suppose. Well, then, can you not find her out, and tell her what has occurred, and that her property is safe at the jeweller's in Queen Street?"

"Certainly, sir—of course the first thing is to get the bracelet back to its owner. Norah must go with me to our priest, and, perhaps, if she describes the lady, he'll know who it is, or help us to find out. I'm sure, sir, I'm thankful to you for saving her from being locked up; it 'd most have broke my heart."

" Well, well, it's very sad—very sad, indeed," said the old gentleman. "I hope she'll be a better girl, and never do these things again. 'Honesty is the best policy,' as the old saying is, and no good ever comes from falsehood and deceit. But I must give you a trifle towards a Christmas dinner," he added, putting some silver into the woman's hand, who took it thankfully. Then saying a few kind words to Norah, bidding her to be a good child in future, he went downstairs and home, thinking a great deal of what he had seen.

" Well, this is a trouble I never thought to have, Norah," said Mrs. Brian, when they were alone again. "You'll just come round to his reverence, and see what he's got to say to all this."

" Oh, mother, I can't—I'm afraid. I can't bear him to know about it."

" I should have thought it was the least you could do now, Norah, and that you'd want to make things right as soon as you could."

" Yes, mother," stammered Norah, "I do. I'll go to confession on Christmas-eve, mother: won't that do?"

" Yes, of course you'll go then, but you must

come to Father Russell now, for me to find out what I've got to do.   I couldn't eat my dinner on Christmas—which, thanks to this gentleman, we'll have—it'd really come nigh to choke me, I do believe, if I hadn't done all I could to get the lady her bracelet back."

So, very unwillingly, Norah went with her mother to the priest's house, and stood silently, and almost sullenly by, whilst he was hearing the tale.   Poor child, she wasn't really sullen, but she was trying hard to be "brave," as she thought it, and not cry there, with Father Russell and her mother looking at her.

If the priest had scolded her, I think Norah would have grown hard and proud, perhaps; but when he looked as kind as ever, and said, "Poor child! how unhappy you must be with all these stains upon your soul!" she just dropped down on her knees, and covering her face with her hands, sobbed out, "Oh, Father, I'm miserable.   I've been miserable ever since the night I took the bracelet, and I'm sorry, and I want God's pardon."

"Then, Norah, if you are really sorry you will go to this lady to-morrow.   I can tell you her name and address, and you will speak the whole truth, and ask her forgiveness: then come to your confession, so that Christmas morning may dawn upon you with your sins washed away by the precious Blood of Christ."

Norah promised obedience, and went home with her mother, but although the old gentleman's gift had come as a great help to them, they were a very silent little group in that upstairs room, for Brian was vexed and cross, Mrs. Brian sad and tearful, and Norah thoroughly humbled and ashamed; whilst the younger children had a sort of idea that something was wrong, and got together in a corner to whisper and wonder, and look suspiciously at their elder sister.

Next day Norah got up and went her rounds, as usual, early in the morning, but all the while she was thinking of what was before her in the afternoon—the terrible punishment of going to this Mrs. Harrison, whom Father Russell knew quite well, and giving her the history of the lost bracelet.

By the time the clock struck three they were at the door. Norah would have gone down the street once again to get courage, if she had been alone, but her mother rang the bell and gave her no time for delay. Five minutes after they stood in a large room before Mrs. Harrison, and it was the most terrible moment Norah had known during all her life.

" You come from Father Russell ?" inquired the lady. "Sit down. Can I do anything for you ?" Norah looked at her mother, and her mother returned the look, but neither of them spoke.

" It's my girl, Norah, here," said Mrs. Brian, at last. " You're the lady who lost a bracelet, and she can tell you where it is and all about it."

" Oh, I am very glad," said Mrs. Harrison, " I prize it very much; I thought it was quite lost. If Norah, as you call her, has found it, she deserves a reward, and I must give her one."

" Oh, no, no !" cried Norah. "I saw you drop it a-getting into the cab, and I wouldn't tell. I know I ought, but I didn't, and I picked it up when no one was looking ; and I meant to sell it, to get food and clothes." And there she broke down and looked at her mother, who took pity on her, and helped her tell the rest, until it was all out.

" How strange it was," Norah said, after, " that any one should be so kind." Even Mrs.

Harrison seemed more sorry than angry, sorry that Jesus should have been grieved by Norah's unfaithfulness.

"Don't you say your prayers, my dear ?" she asked. "Do you not know that when we are tempted to do wrong, God will always help us to get away from the evil thought, if we ask Him?"

" Yes, I know; but I didn't do it," said Norah. "I will, though. I'll never do such a thing again—never."

" You think so now, Norah, because you are feeling all the shame which has come on you. But you are a child, and you will be tempted over and over again to do wrong—we all are. Will it keep you safe if you trust to yourself ? Can't you do something better ?"

"I can say a ' Hail Mary,' or make the sign of the Cross," said Norah.

" Yes; one little prayer to our Blessed Lady would help you to keep away from sin; one sign of the Cross would surely keep you from grieving Jesus, Who died for you. You wouldn't have taken my bracelet and hidden it, and kept it all those weeks, if you had seen Our Lord by your side, looking into your face all the time, Norah ?"

"Oh, no, no! I didn't think of all that. I knew it was wrong, but I forgot about Him," sobbed Norah.

"Well, now try to be very sorry and promise Him you won't forget Him so easily. I forgive you, quite; and I shall come and see you some day, to find out how you are going on."

A great weight was off Norah's mind as she came away from Mrs. Harrison's. She had never expected any one would be so kind to her, and then in the evening she went to receive God's pardon for her sin; so that Christmas-day found her happier than had seemed likely a few days before.

But Norah had a good deal to suffer, for her father reproached her continually with what she had done.

"I never thought a girl of mine 'd turn out a thief," he would say ; and then Norah would cry bitterly, for it seemed so hard to hear of her sin again and again, when she hoped God had forgiven her.

"You must bear it patiently," the priest said to her once, when she complained of her father's unkindness. "Though God has I hope forgiven you, He means you to suffer some punishment for having offended Him. It is because He loves you, Norah, and wishes you to learn the consequences of breaking His laws, that He lets this trouble you."

Norah could not say anything then. She knew that after all she was bearing much less than she deserved; but as week after week her father kept reproaching her, her brothers and sisters telling her of what she had done, and even the boys and girls in the court running after her with the cry of "thief," she sometimes wished she could get away where nobody knew her, and begin quite afresh to be a different girl. But Mrs. Harrison had watched her, and finding that Norah was trying to be honest and respectable, she resolved to put the girl to school, so that she might be trained to get her living in some better and safer way than in the streets of London, as a watercress-seller. It was awkward at first. Norah could bargain for oranges, or tie up watercresses in bunches, and cry them in her shrill, clear voice, from morning to night; but she could not master the difficulties of reading and writing for ever so long; and as for sewing, it would have been a hopeless task to any but the patient nuns who instructed her—the handling of watercresses and needles was so very different. But in time the difficulties grew less, and Norah was softening down wonderfully from the rough slipshod girl who had once scampered about Spencer's-court, and the streets and alleys near it.

"She's a good girl now," Mrs. Brian would say; "never thinks of herself, but is always ready to help with the little ones. I always wanted to take her out of the streets if I could, but it was more than I could manage."

Four years later, if you had gone into a pleasant house a few miles out of London, about eight o'clock in the morning, you might have seen a bright-faced dark-eyed nursemaid in the midst of a troop of little children, fresh and rosy from their morning bath. They all loved "Norah," with her merry songs, and pleasant voice, and gentle patient ways, and she is as fond of them as ever she was of the little rough-headed, unwashed brothers and sisters in Spencer's-court. For it is really Norah Brian—once the dirty watercress-girl

—now so neat, so trim, and so respectable. It is a great change, but not much to be wondered at if you knew the change in her heart —the love to God, the constant effort to keep His commandments and be a faithful child of His Holy Church, which began to spring up gradually out of the true sorrow which followed upon that early sin.

GOOD FOR EVIL.

HE prettiest cottage in all Sedgefield was John Miller's; but the garden, with its lilies, and roses, and hollyhocks, was even more to be admired, and this was Bessie's care—her one great happiness after school-hours were over and home-work was done. Very early in the morning Bessie would get up and dress and say her prayers, and then steal softly downstairs, so that she should disturb no one, on purpose to weed, and rake, and water; to tie up the flowers which the wind had blown too roughly, or gather the fruit which she managed to sell to some of the families who lived near; and I can tell you that Bessie Miller was a happy girl when she could hand her mother a few shillings which she had earned from her own work in the garden.

But one summer, Bessie could not help fancying that her flowers disappeared strangely in the night. She would look at them the last thing before she went to bed, to reckon on what would be ready for gathering next morning, and yet, when morning came, some were gone.

"It's your fancy, child," said her mother, when Bessie complained of this. "Who would take your flowers, when all the village knows why you work so? There isn't one of our neighbours would be so mean." However, it soon became quite clear to all in the cottage, that Bessie was right. Her flowers were certainly taken in the night; but no foot-marks could be found, and it seemed impossible to guess who was the thief.

"I'll watch," said Bob, the eldest of the family. And so he did; sitting up after the rest at night, and getting down earlier than even Bessie; but still no one could be seen, and yet lilies, roses, pinks, and pansies from the beds, and jasmine and honeysuckle from the walls of the cottage were disappearing like magic.

At last, one morning, Bessie found it all out. She had risen before it was broad daylight to pick strawberries to take to the Squire's house for breakfast, and as she stepped about carefully amongst the plants, lifting the leaves to find the red berries, she heard a rustling in the laurel hedge close by, and as she started and raised her head, a girl ran out into the road, dropping flowers as she flew along in her haste, which Bessie recognised as her own. She was a big girl, rough-headed and dirty, with neither shoes nor stockings on her feet, but, though older and larger, she could not distance Bessie, who was running after and came up with her in a few minutes.

"My flowers! my flowers!" cried Bessie, breathlessly. "You bad girl! You thief, you! Why did you steal from me?"

"I'm poor—well-nigh starved. I wanted 'em to sell," said the girl, sullenly.

"But they're not yours," said Bessie. "*I'm* poor; there's so many of us that I want to earn money to help mother. How could you be so wicked as to take my flowers?"

"Poor!" sneered the girl; "I'd like to know what you'd say to our place—where my

little brother's lying and crying for food.   He
wants bread, and I've none to give him, and he
groans and cries, and I can't bear it.   You'd steal
flowers, or anything else you could sell, if you
was me."

Bessie looked at the girl.   Yes, she certainly
had a ragged, starving look.   " Don't your
father and mother work for you ?" she asked.

" Mother's dead, since Harry was 'most a
baby.   Father only beats us, and kicks us; and
sometimes he's at work and sometimes not."

Bessie was cooling down then.   She had
been very angry, but now she was getting to feel
sorry for the miserable-looking girl at her side.

" You can keep these flowers you've got in
your apron," she said, gravely.

" Lor! I mean to, you may be sure, " answered
the other, laughing.   " You didn't suppose a
little slip of a thing like you'd get them from
me, did you ?"

Bessie's face flushed.   She couldn't' bear to be
laughed at.   " I could ask my father or Bob to
come after you," she answered, " but I'm not
going to.   I'm sorry for you because you are so
poor and unhappy, and I'm sorry for your little
brother."

"Well, then, give me some of them strawberries I see growing over yonder in the leaves.
I watched you picking of 'em; I meant to get
some for Harry."

" You mustn't steal them," said Bessie. " If
you'll be a good girl, and leave my garden alone,
I'll ask mother to let me come and see you and
Harry, and bring him some fruit, shall I ?"

The girl nodded. " I lives over the common,
there's no house near ours, you can't mistake ;
it's a tumble-down sort of place, and all the
windows is broke, so you'll know; my name's
Nelly Morris."

" Well, I'll come if mother 'll let me," said
Bessie. " Good-bye ;" and she went back to her
strawberry-picking till breakfast was ready,
but all her thoughts were with Nelly Morris and
her little brother.

"Mother, I caught the girl who steals my
flowers. She comes very early—before it's
hardly light, and she sells them, mother. She's
got such a wretched home, and her little
brother's crying for bread, and their father beats
them and half starves them."

When Bessie Miller said this, there was a
general questioning and exclaiming from father

mother, brothers, and sisters: Bob said if he, only caught the thief, "he'd pitch into her, " while Mrs. Miller wanted to know her name, and where she lived, and all about her.   But when Bessie owned to having promised Nelly Morris to go and see her, to take her fruit, too—fruit which would sell for money—they talked still more, and wondered what had come to Bessie.

"Take fruit to them as robs us, child ?" said the father.   "That's a queer sort of way to do. I'm going to try and lay hands on her and give her something to remember. "

"Oh, father, don't !" cried Bessie.   "I was so angry at first, I'd like to have seen her punished then.   But when she told me of Harry, her little brother, her face looked quite different, and I'm sure there were tears in her eyes.   She wouldn't steal if it wasn't that he's well-nigh starving."

"A parcel of lies I'll be bound," cried Mrs. Miller.   "Morris ? I don't know the name; I daresay there's no such person living near, but I'll find out."

The first chance she had of inquiring was not far off, for in less than an hour, as Mrs. Miller stood nursing the baby at the garden-gate, the priest passed by and stopped for a moment to speak to her and notice Bessie's flowers.

" Yes, she takes a rare sight of trouble with 'em, Father. She earns mostly three or four shillings a week, now it's summer-time, between her flowers and the strawberries. She's a good girl, too, though she's got her faults, Father."

"Well, we all have those," said the priest; " but I hope Bessie tries to be good."

" She's so queer about things, sometimes," continued Mrs. Miller. " She's been fretting and fussing for a month back, because some one's been stealing her flowers; and now she's found out who it is, nothing will do but she wants to go and see the girl and take some of her strawberries."

" It isn't one of our village girls, I hope ?" said Father Joseph.

" It's a girl called Morris, Bessie tells me, Father. She says she lives over the common ; you don't know the name, I suppose ?"

" Yes, there are Morrises live in the cottage there. The mother died six years ago, at least, and I visited her. She had been a Catholic in her childhood, and when she was dying she sent for me, but it was a sad end. Her husband is a worthless drinking fellow—a Protestant, and the children are Protestants. I have tried

12—2

again and again to get to see them, but he will not admit me."

" Well, it's there Bessie wants to go, Father—after this girl's been stealing from our garden too. She shan't go near them, though."

" It would be returning good for evil, Mrs. Miller, and she might teach this poor girl something. I think I would let her go once were I you."

So next day Bessie picked a few strawberries and some of her flowers and started for Nelly Morris's home. She wasn't at all sure that Nelly had not been at the garden again ; however, she would go and see little sick Harry, now her mother had given her leave.

Certainly the Morrises' home was easy to find. No other cottage was near, and the windows were broken and stuffed with rags, and it looked as miserable as the girl had described.

Bessie tapped at the door, but no one answered; she heard a pitiful crying voice as she stood listening, and she guessed it was little Harry. Perhaps he was alone, so she pushed open the door. Everything was as wretched as could be. There was scarcely anything in the room, and down in the corner, on a small mattress, a little boy of about seven years was lying, his tangled hair nearly covering his face, his eyes filled with tears, and his arms tossed out on the blanket which covered him whilst he kept up his pitiful cry of weariness and pain.

Bessie went near and the child looked eagerly at the basket she carried; but when she spoke he grew shy and turned away his head.

" Harry, don't cry. I've got something nice for you," said Bessie.

No answer; but the crying ceased.

"Harry, look at me! I told Nelly—your sister Nelly—I'd bring you some strawberries see!" Harry peered out through his tangled hair, and a smile shone over his dirty little face, and then he sat up and ate the strawberries one by one, as Bessie handed them to him, until only a few were left.

" Keep 'em for Nell," Harry, said then, looking into the basket; "she never has anything nice, she'll like 'em ever so."

"Where is she ?" asked Bessie.

" She's gone to Granny's, over in the town, to see if she'll give us anything. She'll be in directly," and that minute the latch was lifted, and "Nell" appeared, as dirty, ragged, 'and slip-shod as ever. She took no notice of Bessie, only went straight to the little mattress and knelt down by the sick boy with a look of love in her eyes which one could never have imagined. Many a time the remembrance of it checked Bessie when she was cross or quarrelsome with *her* little brothers at home.

" Here, Harry ; Granny's sent you this," she said, picking out a piece of bread from the rest she had in her pinafore ; but Harry pushed it aside and held out his hand for the flowers Bessie gave him.

" She's brought me these, Nell, and straw-berries, and there's some left for you. I like her."

The girl turned to Bessie then, "Thank you," she said, " I'm glad you've come. I won't touch your things no more. I took a few this morning — they weren't many, though. I wouldn't have done it, only there was nothing in the house, and I sold 'em for fourpence, and got some tea for Harry. I'll not go again though. Granny's given me twopence, and these bits of bread, and we'll get on for a day or two, and perhaps father will come home then."

"Is your granny good to you?" asked Bessie.

"No, she's cross, and I hate her," said Nelly. "She lives a way off, but I go and beg a penny from her when I can. She's poor, too."

" Where's your father ?"

" Oh, he's gone off these three days. There's a fair somewhere, and I s'pose he's gone."

" Do you go to school, Nelly ?"

"School! no, I should think not, indeed. What's the use of it ?"

" Why, can you read ?"

" Yes, just a bit—as much as I wants to."

Bessie couldn't understand such a girl as this; she hardly knew what to say next, so she felt it was time to go home.

"Good-bye, Nelly," she said; "good-bye, Harry. I'll come again if you like ; and would you like a picture ?"

The little boy's face said "yes," though he did not speak ; but when Bessie was gone he talked of her and her pleasant look, and clean frock, and the strawberries and flowers, till Nelly was half-angry.

"You care more for her than you do for me," she cried, jealously.

"I don't," said Harry. "You're good to me, Nell, and I love you best of every one : but couldn't you have your face as clean as hers ? I'd like to see you look pretty, too."

Nelly declared she didn't want to be clean, and didn't want to be pretty, but, for all that, she took the hint, and two days after, when Bessie went to the cottage, she was surprised to see that the girl had not only a clean face, but that she had made some attempt at smoothing her own hair and Harry's.

This time Bessie Miller had had no difficulty to get her mother's consent to go to the Morrises cottage. "Poor things," she had said, when Bessie described their misery, "maybe you might be some use to them. If you could only get the girl to the Catholic school, now, it would be a fine thing. His reverence was right, to be sure —you may go again if you like."

Bessie *did* like — she had taken a fancy for little sickly Harry, and she felt a great pity or Nelly, though she was so dirty, and rough and dishonest; so she picked a few more straw-berries, and took a little picture with her, one which she felt sure Harry would like, and which she had treasured up at home for a long, long while. It was the picture of Jesus, as the Good Shepherd, with the little lamb upon His shoulder, which He is carrying over the rough steep path; and when Bessie looked at it she wished she knew how to tell Harry that Christ was taking care of him, just like that; perhaps it would keep him from crying so badly.

So when the strawberries were finished, this picture was brought out, and Nelly drew near to look as Bessie knelt down by Harry to tell him all about it.

"See," she said, "it's a poor little lamb. The thorns and brambles have torn it, and it's all bleeding and hurt, and the Good Shepherd has come and lifted it on His shoulder to carry it to the sheep-fold."

" My! isn't it pretty?" said little Harry, drawing a deep breath. Nell stared, but said nothing.

"It means something more, though," said Bessie.   "The Good Shepherd is Jesus, and we are like His lambs, us children.   He will take us in His arms and keep us safe till we get to heaven at last, if we'll let Him, you know."

Neither Nell nor Harry *did* "know."   Their vacant stare at Bessie showed that, and she did not quite understand how to make it plain to them.

"Who is He ?" said Harry.

"Jesus Christ—God," answered Bessie.

"Oh, He's the one as sends bad people to hell, isn't He ?" said Nelly.   "The parson told me that once ; he said I'd go there safe."

"Oh, Nelly, I hope not.   It's a dreadful place, and bad people *will* go there ; but then Jesus will be very sorry, for He wants them to go with Him to heaven.   No one goes to hell except they choose to be bad."

"Why should He care ?   What makes Him sorry ?" said little Harry.

"Oh, He loves us all so," answered Bessie. "Like Nelly loves you, Harry, only better."

"He *don't !*" cried Nell, angrily.   "No one loves Harry half as much as I do.   Go away, do ; I don't want you here.   Go away !"

Poor Bessie ! She had done her very best, and yet she had made Nelly cross. Half frightened at the girl's sudden passion, she was going away without a word, only Harry stopped her. "Come again," he said, holding out his little wasted hand; " come and tell me some more — I like to hear it. Never mind Nelly, she don't mean any harm; she's cross now, but she'll be sorry by-and-by. You see she can't bear to think any one would love me better than she does."

"Good-bye," said Bessie ; but she did not say she would come again. In a different way she was almost as angry as poor Nelly, and as she went home her thoughts were after this kind :

"I won't go near the girl. She stole my flowers, and I forgave her ; and I've been good to her and Harry, and she is not one bit thankful to me ; and then, when I was telling them about Our Lord, and meaning to teach them nicely, she spoke to me like that. I won't have it !"

"Pride, Bessie," whispered conscience. "You were pleased with yourself for being kind;

you were thinking how finely you were getting on, and what a good girl you were."

"I wasn't." Oh, how she disliked that troublesome voice of conscience just then! "I wasn't thinking anything of the kind." Yet, the next feeling was, that conscience had said the truth; that was why it was so very disagreeable.

However, for all the rest of the evening, Bessie Miller was in a bad mood. Nothing went right.

"Have you been to the Morrises?" asked her mother.

"Yes, and I shan't go any more. I can't bear that Nelly."

It was such a new, strange tone, that Mrs. Miller stared in surprise.

"Why? What's wrong? What's she been up to?"

"Oh, nothing, mother; can't you let me be?" said Bessie, pettishly; and she ran straight upstairs, and never showed her face till she was called to get the little ones to bed. Then she was so cross that they grew naughty and tiresome, and Bessie scolded, and slapped, and talked angrily—they *did* have a time of it; and their mother, who heard something was wrong, said to herself, over and over again: "Whatever ails the child? I haven't seen her in such a temper I don't know the day when."

You will not wonder that when Bessie went upstairs that night she was not at all happy. The little ones who shared the same room were asleep, and when she glanced at their rosy, peaceful faces, she wondered how she could have been so unkind. Even Nelly Morris, who knew nothing to make her good, would not strike or scold Harry—Bessie was sure of that, since she had watched the look of love in her eyes as she stooped over him. Poor Nelly! whom she had felt almost to hate since she had spoken so roughly to her. Ah! that was the beginning of her own temper; she had been put out then, and all had gone wrong since. Yet, Bessie felt particularly disinclined to kneel before her little crucifix and ask God's pardon; the pride in her heart was trying to hold her back from doing the one thing which would set her right again. She fidgeted about—at last she got into bed, and resolved to go to sleep and think no more about it;

every one was cross sometimes, it wasn't a great sin. But it was no use; in five minutes Bessie was on the floor, saying her usual night prayers only: saying them though, in a hasty, careless way, to feel they were done. But when she came to the words, " Forgive us our trespasses," she stopped quite short. She hadn't forgiven Nelly ! no, and she *couldn't*, it was too bad. Not forgive a poor, ignorant girl for vexing her? Another minute, and Bessie was sorry, with all her heart, for her silly pride, and passion, and ill-temper, and begging God to pardon her for what she had done to grieve Him. She could lie down quietly, then, though she was still so sorry; and she was thinking how she would go to the Morrises' cottage next day and be extra kind, and how she would be more gentle to the little ones, to make up for her ill-temper, when she fell asleep till it was morning, and her first waking thought was to ask God to help her to keep her resolutions.

"I'm sorry I was cross last night—it was too bad of me, when you'd been good to Harry," said Nelly Morris, rather awkwardly and shyly, when Bessie came to the door next day. It cost her a struggle to bring it out, but she had promised Harry, for he had cried half the night with the fear that Bessie, pictures, and strawberries, were lost to him for ever.

"Never mind," said Bessie, feeling rather awkward, too; "you didn't mean it I know. How's Harry?"

"He is not so well, he's been fretting so;" and the tears welled up into the girl's eyes. "He thought you'd not come."

"You didn't promise. I asked you, and you didn't say yes," struck in the child, in the half sad, half whining tone, that had become usual with him.

How Bessie blushed! She had shown temper, then, to these children, whom she wanted to teach to love God. They must indeed see she was no better than themselves; but the thought kept her humble and when Harry began to ask her about the picture again she wasn't thinking so much of herself as she explained it to him.

"I've brought some more, Harry—some of mother's. I can't give them to you, but I thought you'd like to look." There were several which the boy admired very much but he turned back to his own "Good Shepherd," declaring that he liked it much the best of all.

" I'd like to see Him a-carrying the lamb," said Nelly ; " He's got a kind face."

" O yes !   All the pictures of Our Lord have got a kind face because He *was* so good and gentle."

" I don't know about Him," said Harry; "tell me more."

" Why, He was up in heaven, Harry, and though it was so bright and beautiful He left it to come down in the world to die for us. And He was so good to every one—He never turned any one away, and He cured the people who were sick, and forgave those who were sorry for their sins, and He loved little children most of all, I think, for He took them up in His arms and blessed them.".

" Who told it you ?   Are you sure it's true ?'

" Why, we learn it at school and at church. The priest tells us, and of course it's true, because Jesus has put him here on purpose to teach us such things."

Nelly looked suspiciously at Bessie. "You're a Catholic, then," she said. "Father hates 'em, and he hates the priests. Wouldn't he be angry if he caught you here!"

"No," said Harry; "he wouldn't know anything about it, and she *shall* come, Nelly. I don't care what she is: I like her."

"Do you hate Catholics too, Nelly?" said Bessie.

"N—no, not exactly. I don't like any one scarcely, 'cept you; and I didn't like you last night, either, 'cause I thought you wanted Harry to love Him in the picture more 'n me."

"Well, I do," said Bessie; "but then, Nelly, I ought to want Harry to love Jesus Christ, so that he can go to heaven some time, and never have any pain, or be ill."

"Ah! I'd love Him if He'd keep me from feeling bad," muttered Harry, half to himself; but his sister looked glum—she didn't like it yet.

It was a long hot walk across the common, but Bessie Miller did not mind very much; and gradually she and little Harry became great friends, and most of her spare time was spent with him, reading, singing to him, or showing him pictures. Nelly was sometimes there and sometimes not; but she had left off feeling jealous of her little brother's liking for Bessie. It pleased Harry so to have her come, that Nelly grew to feel quite disappointed for him when a day went by without his visitor appearing.

The summer was passing. Strawberries were over, and flowers and fruit were growing scarce; yet Bessie often found some for Nelly Morris to sell, and also to give as presents to Harry. Certainly she had fewer for herself, and so she earned less money; but her mother was willing to give up a little, if it was the way of doing good to these poor children; and very often too she would send them bits of meat and bread, which she could ill spare. But though Bessie saw the little boy very often, she was quite sure that there was a change in his face, and that his little hands grew thinner, and his eyes larger and brighter. One day Nelly followed her to the door, saying, "Don't he seem worse than he used to be?"

Bessie stopped still a moment, then she said, "I think—I'm afraid he's not going to live long, perhaps."

The tears came into Nelly's big dark eyes.

"If he dies, I'll die too!" she cried. I won't live without him!—he's all I've got since mother died. And I've loved him, and done for him, and thought of nothing else, and if he dies!—oh, he can't; he shan't!" and Nelly rushed back into the miserable cottage without another word, whilst Bessie went sorrowfully home to tell her mother.

"It'd be a blessed thing if the little lad was took, that is, if one could get the priest to baptise him," said Mrs. Miller. "Couldn't you get the girl to let Father Joseph see him?"

"I don't believe she'd dare, mother; her father hates the priests so, and though he's mostly away, he does come home sometimes, and Nell never knows when he'll turn up. But I'll ask her, mother."

So next visit Bessie paid to the cottage, she got Nelly to come to the door when she was leaving, and then she said, "Do you know if Harry's been christened anywhere?"

The girl shook her head. "Dunno," she replied: "what is it?"

"Well, did your father ever have him took to church when he was little, and have water poured over him when they gave him his name?"

"No," said Nell, in very great astonishment. " Father's never had him took to church, that I'm certain ; 'tain't likely."

"But he ought to be baptised. He won't live long, Nelly, I'm sure he won't ; and, you see, he'll never, never be with Jesus in heaven if he's not baptised."

Nelly's face grew hard and angry. "Don't tell me, like the parson did, as Harry'll go to hell. I won't believe it. What harm's he done, I'd like to know ?"

" I never said it, Nelly," cried Bessie eagerly. "I hope Harry wouldn't go to such a terrible place; but if he was only a little baby, just born, he couldn't live with Jesus in heaven unless he'd been baptised."

" *Stuff !*" said Nelly. "Who said it ? Why shouldn't he ? I thought you told Harry as this Jesus you're always talking about loves him !"

" And it's true—Jesus loves him dearly. He wants Harry to be in heaven ; and yet He has said none can go there who hasn't been washed white by baptism. O Nelly, can't you have it done ?"

Nelly hesitated. "The parson wouldn't

come; he's been often to get us to his school, but he's done with us long ago."

"Oh, I didn't mean him.   A priest can do it best, Nelly, and Father Joseph would come."

"I know, him—he's called here, too; but father wouldn't have him in, and he said if I let him come he'd half kill me if he found it out."

"Does your father know Harry's so ill ?" asked Bessie.

"No; he's not been home much, and when he is, he's the worse for drink, and don't notice. He'd be cut up enough if Harry died; he'd be sorry then he hadn't treated us different."

It certainly seemed very hopeless : evidently Nelly dared not admit the priest against her father's orders, and there was small chance of such a man consenting to have the dying boy baptised.   However, all the Millers began to pray to the Blessed Virgin for Harry, and then they felt sure in some way she would answer them.

Perhaps it was a week after that, when Bessie went to the cottage one day, she saw the girl holding Harry in her arms.   He was too restless and weary to stay on his mattress, and his face had the signs of death upon it.

Bessie went close and took one small hand in hers, and then the boy whispered, "Sing me something—I'd like it."

"Yes," said Bessie, with tears rolling down her cheeks; "what shall I sing?"

"The one I like—about the Good Shepherd."

So Bessie began, in a trembling, unsteady voice, the hymn she had sung by Harry's side many a time before: "I was wandering, and weary;" and Harry smiled as he listened, and said over some of the words after her, but he soon grew tired even of that, and leaned his head wearily on Nelly's shoulder. Bessie stayed as long as she could, but at last she went, leaving Nelly clasping her little brother in her arms, all alone in the wretched cottage.

"Mayn't I bring Father Joseph?" she whispered. "Mayn't I bring mother to stop with you?"

But Nelly shook her head; so Bessie went crying over the common towards her home, saying "Hail Marys" all the time, for Harry.

Now and then the boy would raise his head and ask for water, and talk of Bessie, of his picture, of Jesus the Good Shepherd, in a rambling sort of way. "He'll take me to heaven; He'll come—Bessie said so; she said He would if I'd let Him;" and then he would seem to sleep again. Then the shadows fell, and darkness crept into the room, and Nelly could not move to get a light, Harry grasped her so tightly. Then came a footstep to the door.

"What, dark;" cried an angry voice. "A nice home to come to! Harry! Where are you, I say?"

"Father, we're here; I'm holding Harry; he's bad."

"Put him down, girl, and get a light."

"He's dying, father."

Morris stood still. Then he came stumbling and groping his way towards the children, and presently found a match and struck a light. Ah, what a cry he gave as he glanced at the boy. It was more than three weeks since he had seen him, and it was a terrible change since then.

"Harry! Harry!" he said; "here's father. Give him me, Nell. Oh! Harry, I've been cruel and bad to you, but say you'll forgive me."

But Harry never answered, only drew closer to his sister, and rambled on again about "Bessie, and flowers, and the Good Shepherd."

"What's he talking of?" asked Morris.

"It's some one who's been kind to him, father; a girl who's brought him things, and given him pictures ; he's thinking of her."

" Why didn't any one tell me he was bad ?" exclaimed the father. " I never knew he was going to die. Can't some one do him good ?"

A sudden thought struck Nelly. She remembered Bessie's words, and now was the time to brave her father's anger if it was true that it would be well for Harry.

"Father, there is only one thing he wants. He's always talking of going to heaven and not feeling any pain."

"Don't talk that way to me ! I don't believe such things, girl."

" But Harry does, father—he wants the Good Shepherd to take him. And, oh, father ! he can't ever go there, he can't ever be in heaven, Bessie says, unless—unless——"

"Unless what ?" shouted Morris. "Don't you hear how he's breathing ?—don't you see he's going fast ?   Let's hear what he wants, and I'll do it."

" Let the priest come, father, that's all."

A terrible oath was on Morris's lips, but something checked him.

"I've swore that him and the like of him shall never cross my way; but if Harry wants him, he may come. I'll clear out, I'll get anywhere —it don't matter. Let me hold the boy while you run for him, and then I'm off. Harry'll be dead, and I don't care what becomes of me."

Quick as a dart, Nelly rushed to the Millers' cottage—her dress more disordered than usual, her hair streaming in the wind—but she never knew or cared.

"The priest! the priest!" she cried, as Mrs. Miller opened the door. "Fetch him quick, father says so; and tell Bessie to come, for Harry's dying." And she was gone again, for what *should* she do if he died without her?

He was living, though breathing heavily, and lying almost unconscious in his father's arms, yet when Nelly took him he opened his eyes and smiled. "Bessie! my picture!" he murmured.

More footsteps at the door. It was Mrs. Miller, and Bessie, and the priest, who came in. But Morris never stirred: he seemed fixed to the spot, heeding no one, remembering nothing, except that his boy was dying.

A short time, and Harry had been made a

Christian—the stain of original sin and the actual sins of his little life all washed away. The water had revived him, and he was no longer unconscious, but lay very still, and white, and smiling.

"The Good Shepherd has got you safely now," whispered Bessie, who knelt close by him.

Then the priest came nearer, and took one of Harry's little hands in his own. "Jesus will soon take you, my dear little boy. Are you glad?"

"Yes, I'm glad. I'm tired of being so miserable and poor; only I'd like Nell to come."

"She will some day, we hope,"—a great sob from poor Nelly—"God wants you first, Harry."

The boy's eyes closed again, he was dying very fast.

Still Morris stood gazing at the group, as if he was stunned with the sudden shock; he neither spoke nor moved.

"Harry," said the priest again, laying his hand upon the boy's head, "say this after me: 'Jesus, once a little child like me, have mercy on me. I am sorry for my sins, and I wish I had been better. Forgive me, dear Saviour, and take me home to heaven.'"

Harry opened his eyes then, and looked round the room, fixing them at last on his father's face. "Father," he whispered.

Morris heard, and pushing the rest aside, went close to the boy, who was lying now on the mattress again.

"Father, be good to Nell," he murmured.

"Harry! Harry! don't die. I want you, boy —I'll begin afresh—I'll do better—I never meant—" but here the strong, rough man broke down, and his head rested by Harry's.

There wasn't a sound in the room, except Nelly's sobs and Bessie's quieter crying, for several minutes: then the child's face brightened, and the priest, who bent over him, heard him whisper, "In His arms—He's got me—the Good Shepherd;" and then he was gone, gone from pain and crying, and from all the sin and sorrow of life, to the Saviour Who loves little children so well.

A week afterwards, Bessie Miller was standing at the garden-gate one evening thinking of Harry—her flowers always brought him to her mind. She was wondering what had become of Nelly, for since the boy was buried, she and her father had disappeared, and the cottage was left empty. After a while, Bessie went down the lane and into the quiet churchyard, to the corner where there was the little new-made grave. But as she came near, she saw some one was there: it was Nelly, stretched on the grass by the side, talking aloud in her sorrow.

"Oh, Harry, why did you die? Why did you leave me?" she said. "Father's better now, but I want you, Harry!"

Bessie dared not speak, dared not try to comfort her; but when Nelly's sobs grew quieter she drew near, and began putting the flowers she had brought upon the grave. The girl sat up then, and watched her, and when it was done she put her hand out to Bessie. "Good-bye," she said; "I'm going away with father to-morrow—he can't a-bear the place now Harry's dead. You'll come here sometimes, won't you, and bring him flowers?"

Bessie promised. "But won't you ever come back, Nell. Won't I ever see you again?"

Nelly shook her head. "Most like not," she said. "But I shan't forget you," and she put her arm round Bessie and kissed her gently; then she ran down the churchyard-path without another word or look, and was gone out of sight before Bessie could follow her.

"Oh, mother, it's so sad! I thought Nelly Morris would stop in Sedgefield and be baptised too, and learn to be a good Catholic. And she's gone, and perhaps she'll never learn anything now." This was Bessie Miller's regret many and many a time when she was talking to her mother of Nelly and Harry and the old tumble-down cottage over the common, where she had spent so many hours.

"We must let God do things His own way, child," Mrs. Miller would say. "He can bring it right without your help, you may be sure. Just keep on praying to our Blessed Lady, and your prayers won't be lost now no more than they were before."

But it was several years later when Bessie Miller had any news of her old acquaintance. She had prayed for her and left off, and forgotten and begun again, many and many a time before the day came when a letter reached her with a foreign stamp on it, which caused a great excitement in Sedgefield and in the Millers' cottage. As nearly every one round that part came to hear the news, there is no reason to keep the contents of the letter a secret: this is what it said:

"DEAR BESSIE MILLER,—I've not forgot you, though perhaps you've forgot me. We're in America now, and father's left off drink, and we're doing nicely —only I wish we was nearer Harry's grave. I thought you'd like to know as I'm a Catholic now, so I've got some one to write this for me, and it's all thanks to you, because you was kind to Harry and me, though I did take your flowers. So no more at present, from your affectionate

"NELL MORRIS."

Wasn't Bessie pleased! and didn't she hurry up to the priest's house to tell him the good news of Harry's sister! "Thank God!" said Father Joseph, as he folded up the letter. "You see, Bessie, that nothing is ever lost by returning good for evil; and often souls may be gained for our dear Lord through a little act or word of kindness."

As no address was given in the letter, Bessie could not answer it, and tell how glad it had made her. All she can do in remembrance of poor Nelly is to take care of the grave in the quiet corner of Sedgefield churchyard, where Harry was laid to rest, and pray that God may bless her while she lives, and grant her a death as peaceful and happy as that of the little brother she loved so dearly.

JOE RYAN'S REPENTANCE.

T was summer—the heavy rain and the wind which blew across the cemetery made it very cold and cheerless; but Joe Ryan and his mother stayed by the grave which was being filled in so quickly; she, poor woman, crying bitterly for the husband who had just been buried there, and the boy was sad and downcast, for he did not know what would become of them now.

"Don't take on, mother, don't," he said. "I'll be a good boy and work for you—you see if I don't."

Mrs. Ryan looked at him through her tears with the thought that it wasn't much a little could do to help keep her and himself and younger children, who were standing frightened and crying, pulling at her shawl every few minutes to ask her to come home.

In the evening Joe and his mother had a talk together: one thing was certain, they must go into cheaper rooms, and then, if Mrs. Ryan could get some work, and Joe find a place, they might manage to live, although it would be hard enough; as for the little ones, they were not big enough for anything but school.

"And how I'm to keep them in clothes, I can't think," said the mother. "Ah! it's a bad thing to lose a good steady husband, and be left with a lot of children like this;" and she began crying again, and nothing Joe could say or do seemed to give her any comfort.

A week later they moved into another street, where they had heard of two small rooms which were to be had cheap, and Mrs. Ryan had got washing to do and one day's work out every week; there was only Joe to be thought of now.

How hard he tried for something to do I cannot tell you. First he spoke to the priest, who promised to look out for him; and next he began to try himself, by asking at every shop he saw, if they "wanted a boy."

But some said he was too small; others that he wasn't strong enough; some told him that if he had come a week sooner they would have tried him; others were sure there were more boys about than people knew what to do with; many looked at him and gave a short sharp "No" to his questions; a few ordered him to "Go about his business," so that altogether it was discouraging work.

Heavy as Joe Ryan's heart felt as he went home day after day without success, nothing was so bad as when the children ran to question him, or his mother looked up from her work to say, "Any luck?" and looked down again with such a disappointed face. Poor Joe! he was giddy and thoughtless and full of faults; but one very good point was, that he really loved his mother, and wanted to be good and useful to her now father was gone.

They hadn't been too well off when Ryan himself was living, for work had been dull for a long while, and then there was his illness, and they had got behind with the rent while he lay doing nothing; however, friends had helped them get clear of debt, so now if Joe could find work they might manage to make a living.

At last one day, when he went for a stale loaf to the baker's shop not far off, the woman behind the counter stopped him when he had put his money down and was going away. "Are you the boy that asked here for a place, two or three weeks ago?"

"Yes," said Joe, his face brightening up. "I want a place very bad indeed."

"Have you ever been at work before?" said the baker's wife. Joe explained that he had always gone to school, but now his father was dead, and he must be doing something "to help mother."

Mrs. Ward then said she wanted a boy to run errands, sweep out the shop, and do anything else that was given him to do; and after a while, if he behaved himself and got on, he might hope for more wages and to go round with the barrow. So the bargain was made, and Joe was to begin work the next day, and he ran home to tell his mother what had happened, feeling more happy than he had done for a long while.

Things went on pretty smoothly for some time after that. Mrs. Ryan kept to her washing, and Joe to his place at the baker's, and sometimes when she was particularly good-humoured, his mistress would give him a stale loaf to take home to his mother and the children, which came in very handy, often enough, when they would have run short of food without it.

Joe's temper was tried a good bit, for Mrs. Ward had a sharp tongue, and now and then she had added a smart blow to the volley of words she had poured out in her anger if he was slow or careless. However, though Joe felt very hot and angry, and very much inclined, as he told his mother, "to pitch something at her head," he never did so far forget himself, but put up with her temper as well as he could, and found that it soon passed away again.

Though she worked hard and late all the week, Mrs. Ryan never made this an excuse for lying in bed on Sunday mornings, and keeping from Mass. She was always regular in her attendance at her church, and saw that her children were the same; and the first time Joe made an excuse for not going, by saying that he "wanted to have a walk," she was more angry than he had ever seen her before.

"Let's have no more of that, Joe!" she said.

"Your father—God rest his soul!—lived and died a good Catholic, and you'll do the same as long as I can keep you to it. Take a walk after if you like, so long as you don't get into bad company; but to Mass you'll go along with me and the little ones, whether you're tired or no, so there!" And Joe, knowing his mother never spoke like that unless she meant it, looked very much ashamed of himself, and said no more. I don't suppose the idea would ever have come into his head, but for another boy, a good deal older, who was also employed at the baker's shop, who had begun to be friendly, and had asked Joe to come out for a walk with him on Sunday mornings. It was not without some difficulty that Joe owned that he went to church with his mother. Poor Joe! his great fault was a fear of being laughed at—a fault which led him into great sorrow afterwards.

"You gander, you!" laughed Smith rudely. "A boy twelve years old going to church with his mother, like a little girl! You'll never be a man at that rate."

Joe coloured up, but still he could not help thinking that his father had gone to church always as regularly as Sunday came round, and nobody could say he wasn't "man" enough.

Smith did not mean to give up the point, though. He teased and talked to Joe every day through one week, until the silly boy had begun to feel vexed with his mother, and inclined to think that she treated him like a baby—not as if he was twelve years old and working for his living. However it was no use thinking to stay away from Mass, that was certain; but Joe made up for it by going long walks with Smith and other lads in the afternoon and evening, instead of being at Catechism or Benediction, as he pretended; indeed he was so anxious not to be hindered from going, that his mother was quite glad to see him "take such a turn," as she said, for she thought that a boy who was so fond of his church couldn't but go on straight and well.

A little time before I don't think Joe could have acted so deceitfully to his mother, and then gone home and looked her in the face, and talked as easily and lightly as he did now; but he had begun to be very clever in turning a deaf ear when his conscience spoke, and so, by little and little, things which once would have felt sins were just nothing at all to him, for he was getting hardened and wicked by degrees.

One false step leads to another, and Joe Ryan found it so, for before long his companion persuaded him that it wasn't any harder or any worse to cheat his master than to deceive his mother, and it was so easy to get a penny or two from the till when he wanted it, to put it back again when it suited him, that Joe did this many a time, until at last he grew less careful about the putting back, and more than once Mr. or Mrs. Ward declared that the money in the till was short, but they never suspected the boy, and, as it was only a trifling sum, the matter blew over for the time. A few peppermints or pear-drops, out of the glass bottles in the window, were nothing to take—so Smith said—and as he was not in the shop at all, but always in the bakehouse, he taught Joe to plunder the biscuit tin and sugar-plums for both of them, persuading him it was all right, and no one thought that sort of thing stealing.

Joe knew better, though ; he knew it was "all wrong," and he knew, too, that these little habits of dishonesty and untruthfulness were growing bigger and stronger every day; and there were times when he felt miserable, and wished from the bottom of his heart that he had never set eyes on Smith.

But he had not the courage to give up his sin. If ever he refused to take what he was asked for, Smith threatened to tell all he had been doing, and the poor foolish boy dared not risk this danger, but fell more and more into his companion's power, by yielding to him oftener through his great fear. When he had first begun to work for his mother, Joe had been regular at his Confession and Communion, and, in spite of many falls and many faults, he had wished and tried to keep out of sin; but since these evil habits had grown up he had kept away from the Sacraments. He knew that to go to them and persevere in his wrong-doing could not be—either occasions of sin must be avoided, or he must do without God's grace; and, sad to say, he chose the last.

This did not happen without his mother noticing it. Week after week she would remind him, and say, "Joe, it seems to me it's a long time since you went to your Confession. Hadn't you best go to-night?" But the boy had always an excuse ready; he was *so* tired, or he had to go somewhere for his master, or it was too late, or he would " go next Saturday." However, he still kept away, and at last Mrs. Ryan spoke to the priest.

"I don't know what's come over my Joe, Father,"she said.   "It isn't that I've much fault to find with him, for he sticks to work, and brings home his money as regular as can be. But there's no getting him to Confession; it's ever so long since he has been, to my certain knowledge—him, too, that was once so willing to go.   I can't help thinking there's something amiss with him."

"I met him near the church, a week ago, and I spoke to him then," said Father Hayes.   " I noticed that he was not regular in his duties, but he promised me to come this week; he said he would be certain to do so."

Mrs. Ryan shook her head very sorrowfully. " That's it, Father — that's always the tale. It's ' I'll go next week, mother; it's too late to-night;' and next week comes, and another, and another, and still he keeps away; and I don't know what to do with him."

"I will try and get hold of him again, and

ask him to come," said the priest. "Joe was one of our best boys at school. It's sad if he begins to go wrong. Perhaps he has bad friends?"

"Oh no, Father—that I'm pretty sure he hasn't," said the poor mother. "I never see him speak to scarce any one, and he don't loiter about the streets like many of 'em. Besides, he hasn't time for much else but work."

"What does he do on Sundays?" asked Father Hayes. "He comes to Mass of course, but why is it I never see him at Catechism?"

"Never see him at Catechism, Father!" cried Mrs. Ryan. "Why, he's as regular at his Catechism as Sunday comes round, and all in a fidget to get his dinner and be off. 'I don't want to be late, mother,' he says to me."

But the priest was pretty certain that wherever Joe was on Sunday afternoons, he was not at the church; and Mrs. Ryan went home feeling very anxious and puzzled, trying to satisfy herself with the thought that perhaps amongst so many boys Father Hayes had overlooked her Joe — no doubt he would notice more particularly next time, and find that he had been mistaken.

When the next Sunday came round, Joe Ryan was in his usual hurry to get off as soon as he had finished his dinner; and his mother looked at his face, and, feeling so sure he would not appear as cool and easy if he was tricking her, thought again how great a mistake Father Hayes had been making; shouldn't she like to convince him of it, too! A happy thought struck her. "Joe, shall you be able to get a word with Father Hayes this afternoon?"

"Yes, mother, perhaps," said Joe coolly, "if I wait till Catechism's over, that's to say."

"Well, then, I wish you'd tell him as Mrs. Saunders, next door, is ill, and she'd take it very kind if he'd look in and see her."

"All right, mother, I'll tell him," and Joe was off—not near the church, though, but to the corner of the next street, where he met his friend Smith and three more lads, older and still worse behaved than he was.

"Thought you weren't a-coming, Ryan," said one; "we were near starting without you."

"Couldn't help it," answered Joe: "mother kept me waiting just at the last—she was giving me a message for our priest."

There was a shout of laughter, and no voice

was higher than Joe's own ; for he had got to
think it a clever thing to be able to tell a lie, or
do a deceitful trick unblushingly, as his companions did; all the same, his conscience was
not quite dead yet, and it reproached him
enough just then. But his uneasy feelings
passed away, and after taking his walk, in
which so much was said and done that he knew
to be bad, Joe went home to his mother to say
that the priest would call and see Mrs. Sanders
most likely the next day.

The week went on as usual, but before it
ended Joe had a heavy trouble on his mind.
Smith, who had often forced him to steal small
sums of money before, had now said that somehow or other he *must* have five shillings by the
next Sunday, and that Joe must get them for
him.

" I can't," said the boy. " What a fool you
must be, Smith, if you don't see I couldn't take
as much as that without being found out !"

"None of that talk for me," said Smith.
" Look here, Joe Ryan, you've got to get me
five shillings before next Sunday. Will you or
won't you ?—come, answer me."

"How can I ?" cried Joe. "You know I

would if I could, but it's impossible. Either master or missis would find it out, and then there'd be a pretty row, and I'd lose my place, . and my character in the bargain."

"I didn't know you'd much to lose," sneered Smith, with a look which brought the colour into Joe's face. "Take your choice, though; either do what I tell you or say you won't, and then I'll go to old Ward and let him know a few things that will surprise him."

"You can't," said Joe; "you set me on to do the things; you're as bad as me, or worse, any way."

"Just as you please," continued Smith quietly, as if Joe had not spoken. "It'll be a great bother and worry to me, and you might let me have the money so easy. I'd give it you back next week, as sure as I'm here."

" But, Smith, I don't, I *really* don't see how it's to be done," said Joe, relenting a little ; "a penny or two at a time is one thing, but five shillings is another. It isn't that I don't want to oblige you—it's because I don't see how to do it. I *really* don't, Smith."

The elder boy considered for a moment. "Don't you ever get any money paid at the doors, Joe, or any bills ?"

"Yes; now I go round to some of the houses I get paid by a few of them, but not so much as five shillings."

"No bills paid at the door?"

"No, Smith, except Mrs. Walters, in the Square."

"Well, that'll do; hand me over the money and say she hadn't got change, but she'd call and pay next week—lots of people do that—and then you should have the money by the time I promise you, Joe, as safe as anything."

"But it don't come to five shillings, Smith—it's only three shillings and sixpence this week."

"Well, I'll try and make that do," said Smith. "It's tiresome—very; but I can manage with that; come, hand it over young 'un."

"I shan't get it till to-morrow, Smith; but are you sure you'll let me have the money back next week?"

"Of course I am. I'm not such a sneak as to get you into a scrape and lose you your place, though you seem to think it. Get me the three shillings and sixpence, Joe, and it shall be in your pocket this day week—that'll do, won't it?"

"Yes, just," said Joe. "Oh, Smith, you'll promise, won't you? It would be a bad thing for me and mother if I got found out."

Smith repeated his assurances, and it ended by the money being safely in his pocket before the next night, much to his satisfaction.

But Joe was anything but happy in his mind. He had not much trust in Smith's words, for he had already found the falseness of them in other ways; and yet, through fear, he had not dared refuse.

When Joe was questioned as to why the bill was not paid as usual, he made the excuse Smith had proposed, and was relieved to find that his master expressed neither anger nor surprise, saying nothing.

But Joe knew no more peace. As the days came he longed for them to pass until the week was at an end and the money returned to him.

However, upon the appointed day, Smith had only excuses to offer; he was very sorry, but "he hadn't been able to bring the money," he said; he would return it for certain in a very few days.

Though Joe was very uneasy, there was

nothing possible but for him to resolve he would never get let into such a scrape again, and then to make another apology to his master.

"It's strange," said the baker. "If it was any one else I shouldn't think so much of it, but I've served Mrs. Walters for this four years, and never knew her let a bill run on beyond a week all that time."

He said no more, but Joe fancied he gazed suspiciously at him, and this made him still more afraid, and he begged Smith to keep his word this time, for he was sure Mr. Ward wouldn't take another excuse.

"All right," said Smith carelessly, but not in a way which gave Joe Ryan any great certainty of his returning the money on the promised day.

When Joe went home that evening he looked pale and worried, so that in spite of his assurance that he was only tired, his mother watched him anxiously, thinking he surely must be ill.

"I'll go to bed," he said at length. "I'm awfully tired, and my head aches, but I shall be all right in the morning;" and he went off, but only that he might get out of any further questioning—he was too wretched to sleep.

For hours he lay awake, tossing from side to side, thinking about Smith and the money, and whatever would happen if he did not soon return it; and then, near morning, he slept, but only to dream all kinds of horrible things, and get up looking pale and heavy-eyed.

Each day as it came saw him still anxious and afraid—he almost expected to be called into the shop-parlour and charged with his theft every time his master or mistress spoke his name ; but still Smith only said he would return the money " to-morrow," and laughed at the boy's fears.

" It's all very fine for you to laugh," said Joe, when another week had run out. " Master'll ask me for the money, and what am I to say ? It's too bad, Smith. I've a great mind to go and tell about it, and how you've bothered me."

" Do," said Smith ; " it won't much matter to me, for I'm going to leave in a week or two. You'll find it a bad look-out for yourself, though —no character and no place. What'll your mother say, and that priest you used to talk so much about ?" and he laughed aloud at his own words.

Joe needed no one to remind him of the misery that was coming, he could foresee it quite well —all his own shame, his mother's misery, Father Hayes' grief that he should go wrong like this, after having been taught so well what was right.

"It's fine for you to laugh," he repeated. "Tell me, are you a-going to give back the money or not?"

"No!" said Smith; "I haven't got it, and I don't know when I'll have it, either—so now you know!"

Was Joe surprised? Hardly; for he had learned, before this, how little mercy he could expect from this lad he had called his friend; but he was silent, almost stunned, by having his worst fears come true. What could he do? Borrow the money? No—that was not possible. Say he had lost it?—his master wouldn't believe it. Oh! if he only dared tell all he had done—anything would be better than this constant fear of being found out. But he dared not—Smith would tell how he had taken things from the shop, and pennies from the till, over and over again; and so he went home, feeling more really ill and miserable than he had done through his whole life before.

That night Mrs. Ryan was roused by hearing Joe murmuring and moaning in his sleep, until at last she hurried to his side, to find him burning with fever, and talking wildly about " Smith " and " money," and other things, in strange confusion. When morning came he did not know, her, and was so bad that she sent for both Father Hayes and a doctor, and a weary time of illness followed.

Although poor Joe wandered from one subject to another, he said enough in his unconsciousness for his mother to be quite sure some great worry had happened to make him ill, and she told the priest, with many tears, that she was sure something had been wrong with him. Ah ! how earnestly they prayed then for Joe, that his life might be spared for a fresh beginning, if possible ; or, at any rate, that it might be continued until he had made his peace with God, Whom he had so long neglected and grieved.

A change came at last—a night on which the poor mother had sat up to watch her boy, knowing that it would be a turning-point for better or worse : how earnestly she said her rosary, and begged hard for him to return to consciousness, I could not tell you. When morning came he opened his eyes, and she saw that he knew her again, and she thanked God and the Blessed Virgin that her prayers were heard. Very slowly Joe got better; but besides his weakness, there was something else hindering his recovery—something on his mind, the doctor declared. How to get him to speak was the question. He was still too weak to bear any excitement; but one day, when Father Hayes came to see him, he found Joe in a very sorrowful and softened state of mind, and, after a little persuasion and encouragement, the whole tale came out, from first to last. Joe kept nothing back, and, even in the telling, in spite of his shame, there was a great relief.

"I'd do anything; I'd soon work and pay it back, if they'd trust me," he said. "What worries me so, is to look at mother, and think of her knowing all this, and how it'll grieve her; and then, what's to be done after all this illness, if I'm out of place, and winter coming on, too?"

"If you had only thought of all this before, Joe, what misery you would have saved yourself, and every one," said Father Hayes. "I don't want to reproach you—I know your own conscience is doing that—but I *must* tell you how much you have sinned against God, and that all this trouble has come through your keeping away from the Sacraments. Surely, Joe, you know that, without God's help and God's grace, not one of us could stand against temptation ; and yet you tried to do it."

Joe shook his head. " No, Father ; I knew I couldn't help going wrong when I gave up my Confession. I stopped away because I'd got into a scrape then, and I didn't see my way to breaking off with Smith, and I knew I'd have to if I told you. I've had a lesson this time, though ! If I could get right now, I'd never do such a thing again, never."

" Say, ' with God's help,' Joe, or I shall not think you have learnt a lesson yet. I want you to feel that if you are left to yourself, away from God and the help He wants to give you, you might do the same again and again, or worse."

" I'd rather mother didn't know," said Joe, brushing a few tears from his eyes with the back of his hand. " She's always trusted me so, and it's hard to have to tell her how I've been taking her in and tricking her, all ways. She's thought I brought her all my money, but I haven't.

They raised my wages ever so long ago, and I kept it back, and never said a word; it isn't the money she'll care so much for, it's the deceit that she'll be so sorry about."

"Yes, it is all very sad, Joe; and I am very sorry for your mother, but I am sure it is better for you and for her that you have no secrets from her, but tell her the whole tale. You will be happier afterwards."

Joe hesitated; but after a bit he promised to take the priest's advice, and then Father Hayes went away, having spoken very seriously to the boy about his sin, and the need of his humbling himself very much before God, after such a course of wrong-doing.

When he was gone, Joe looked at his mother, who had returned to the room, and then he looked at the wall, at the window, at the fire— anywhere and everywhere rather than meet her eyes, which were fixed on him with so much happiness in her look.

"You're a deal better since Father Hayes came, Joe," she said. "We'll be having you out and about, and at your work again, soon, please God."

Joe did not answer; he had got to tell his

mother, that was certain—he had given his word; but how should he begin ?   He coughed, he cleared his throat, he turned over once or twice, and had his pillows shaken up, and took his medicine, and yet it didn't get a bit easier.

Mrs. Ryan sat down to some sewing she had got to employ her during Joe's illness, and seemed inclined to talk. "You remind me more of your father, Joe, since you've been ill," she said. "I suppose it's now you're paler and not so stout—anyway, there's a look of him that seems to bring him back to me almost."

Joe's eyes filled, but he turned on his pillow and said nothing.

"If you only grow up like he was, you'll be a rare comfort to me by-and-by," she added, but he couldn't stand that.

"Oh, mother, *don't !*" he cried. "You don't know, you can't think, how badly I've been going on. I've told Father Hayes, and he says I'd best tell you too, and then I'll be happier ; but—but——" and Joe faltered until his mother came and leaned over him, and soothed and comforted him, almost as if he was a little child once more ; and so, in broken words and with many tears, all his tale came out.

Poor Mrs. Ryan ! That her boy, her Joe, should have deceived her so, was terribly hard ; but she hid her own pain, for she saw how much he had suffered, how real his sorrow was, and she believed that this would be a sufficient lesson, and that Joe would be his own better self once more.

If she had scolded, stormed, reproached him, it wouldn't have cut Joe to the heart as her sad face and quiet words did, when she kissed his forehead and said, " I forgive you, my lad ; but of course you've made me very sad. I never thought you'd be one to deceive me," and then went back to her work, stopping now and again to wipe away the tears which rose in her eyes. Then Joe began to feel how selfish, how bad a boy he had been, to cause all this sorrow to the mother whom he had said he would be a help to.

As Joe grew better, and was able to sit up once more, they agreed that his mother should go to Mr. Ward and say what had happened and pay back the money which he had made use of. She could ill afford it, poor woman, out of her hard earnings, and with all the expense of having Joe on her hands; however, she knew it was right, and believed that she should be able to make up the loss some other way. Once or twice Mr. Ward had sent to ask when Joe would be ready to come and speak to him ; and the lad who brought the message, brought also the news that Smith was gone, and there was a new boy in his place, and another instead of Joe, too. "Master couldn't keep the place open for him ; he only wanted to know about one of the bills—something was wrong."

When Mrs. Ryan went back to her room at the top of the house, to tell Joe this, he looked dreadfully afraid. "You'll go for me, won't you, mother ? I wouldn't face him for anything ; besides, I don't know what he'd do about it."

" I'm going to give him back the money, Joe, so I don't suppose he'd do anything. As to what he'll *say*, that's another matter. You can't expect he'll say anything that's very pleasant—it isn't likely."

" You'll go for me, though, won't you, mother?" Joe had said, and his mother promised, though she felt rather sorry to see that the boy was giving in to his old cowardice.

But when Father Hayes heard of the plan, he would not agree to it. Joe was able to go out again ; he had been to church, he had obtained the grace of the Sacraments ; there was no excuse for him not going to his employer himself to return the money and acknowledge his fault.

Joe didn't like it a bit. "It's a shame!" he said to his mother ; "just as if I hadn't suffered for it already. It's very hard and cruel of Father Hayes to say so, and I shan't do it!"

"Ain't you ashamed of yourself, Joe ?" cried his mother ; "speaking like that of a priest, and one who's been so kind to you too, coming here again and again, and helping me so often when you were so bad. I don't know where we'd be now if it wasn't for Father Hayes."

Joe hung his head. Yes, he *was* ashamed of himself, but he had spoken in temper and vexation, not really meaning it ; he knew that the priest was right ; it was a mean, cowardly thing to push his mother forward to screen his own fault ; yes, he would be brave—anyhow, he would *try*.

So one afternoon Mrs. Ryan and Joe went on their errand, and, with a great deal of stammering and stopping, the boy told what he had done, and handing back the three shillings and sixpence said he hoped Mr Ward would overlook it.

Poor Joe! he felt as if he was doing a very noble thing, he almost expected to be asked to return to his place again: but certainly he never looked for the storm of abuse and reproach which the baker and his wife poured upon him.

"It's all along of being a Catholic, I suppose," said Mrs. Ward in conclusion. "A wicked, lying, cheating set they are, I'm told; doing all manner of things, and then confessing them, and getting clear, as they think, ready to go at it again. I never liked 'em, never! But I'd not have another inside my door, I'd shut the shop up first."

"There, Joe, that's most the worst of it all," said Mrs. Ryan, as they went home again; "you've helped give your religion a bad name; I wouldn't have had it happen for a good deal."

"I know, mother; don't tell me of it, don't!" exclaimed Joe. "It's too bad of them to go on at me so. Other boys have been as bad as me many a time, and worse."

"Don't think of that, Joe; you're nothing to do with other boys. *I* don't want to make things hard for you, lad, it isn't likely; but it's no good letting you fancy that you don't deserve what you're getting. But I know you're really sorry, and God knows it too, and things will be brighter by-and-by."

Poor Mrs. Ryan! she had need of all her faith and trust during the next few months. It was a bitterly cold winter that year, and food and firing were dear, and many a time they wanted bread; for Joe could get nothing to do, and the mother's work was barely enough to pay rent and feed and clothe herself and poor children. How often, when Joe saw her pale face, when he heard the little ones cry from cold and hunger, he would think, " Ah, if it hadn't been for me, we'd have been better off;" and then he remembered how he had talked of himself, and how he should help his mother, and save from his wages, perhaps, to buy her tea now and then, or some coals; and then he determined that if ever he was so fortunate as to get to work again, no one should — by God's help — get him to tell another lie, or do a deceitful thing.

The short days and long nights passed at last. Once more it was spring-time, and as the sun shone down upon the streets and courts where the children played, and into the little room where the Ryans were struggling to live, Joe could not help hoping that as all things were brightening, better, brighter days for him might be coming too. He had tried hard to prove to his mother, during that dreary winter, that his repentance was sincere. In spite of all they had borne, he had been patient and uncomplaining, he had helped her in every way he could, and, best of all, his fall and disgrace had brought him nearer to God, for he had lost a great deal of the pride and self-confidence which he had been full of when first he went to work for himself.

Father Hayes had watched him closely, and was sure that his trouble had done him good; and, now that he kept steadily on in a right path, the priest had great hope that Joe's first unfaithfulness would also be the last.

At length a place was heard of, at a gentleman's house, where a boy was needed to clean boots, and knives, and windows, and such things, and upon the recommendation of Father Hayes, Joe succeeded in getting employed. He was better treated and better paid than he had been in his first situation, and after a while he was able to do more to help his mother, and thus to make up for the suffering and pain he had given her. From that time the boy never again fell into the sin which had brought so severe a punishment; he continued to act and live as a good Catholic, and so all things went well. Many a time he was tempted to do wrong, to speak untruthfully, to act dishonestly, to make acquaintances which were dangerous and bad; but the memory of all the troubles he had brought upon himself kept him straight, joined to the help he received by being faithful to his religious duties; and so Joe Ryan's great faults were in time almost forgotten by those who had known of them, but had also known how real, how sincere was his repentance.

ANNIE'S FIRST PRAYER.

T was a December day—cold enough to make every one wrap themselves in their warmest clothing; but not nearly cold enough to keep the poor children who were only half dressed indoors, for there was very little wind, and the sunshine was clear and bright.

One street in the town of Clayford might have been picked out from the rest for its misery and dirt. Heaps of coal-ashes, potato-skins, cabbage-stalks, and rotten apples were in the roadway ; and from the windows of the dingy houses dirty women leaned out and called to their neighbours, whilst children played round the doors.

Here, on a doorstep, Annie Marsh sat, with her bare feet curled up under her frock, watching the little white clouds which skimmed across the sky; thinking of nothing in particular, excepting that she was warm and comfortable just then, and did not feel so hungry as she had been upstairs.

Presently a great rough lad came bouncing round the corner. "Annie Marsh!" he cried.

"Well, Dick?"

"There's all sorts of things a-doing at the new church, down yonder—that there Catholic place."

"What sorts?" asked Annie, looking straight up at the clouds, and not a bit at Dick.

"Why, there's candles, and flowers, and the queerest goings-on you ever did see. And ain't there music!—my goodness, it's capital! You'd best come."

"Don't want to!" said Annie sharply.

"Very well, then, stop where you are! I'm off to see what's on hand now," and Dick went round the corner again like a shot.

Annie sat still; but she began to find out that she *did* want to go and see, after all. Presently her younger brother came down the street. "Jack!" screamed Annie, "where've you been?"

"Down to the new church, along with Dick Turner," shouted the boy.

"Is it a-going on now ?"

"Likely enough, I don't know."

"Well, run and see, there's a good boy."

Jack disappeared, and soon came back to tell Annie that the "lights was put out and the folks was coming away." But she was consoled by hearing that Dick said there would be more "goings-on" in the afternoon.

When the little bell began to ring for service, Annie was sitting on the doorstep again ; and this time she had the baby to nurse and another tiny child by her side, but she did not mean to be hindered. Clutching the baby tighter, and seizing Bessie's hand, she ran as fast as her feet would carry her towards the simple little mission chapel which had been lately built in that town.

There were only a few people going in, but there were many kneeling inside, as Annie could see in the half-twilight of the winter's afternoon ; and they were lighting candles as she pushed her way in, and her friend Dick nudged her with his arm and asked in a loud whisper if it wasn't "first rate."

Annie did not answer him, but stood still just inside the door, with her big eyes opened to their widest extent. It was so new and strange that she had nothing to say about it just then, only she felt that it was bright and pleasant, and she liked to be there. Presently there was singing—such singing as those ragged children had never heard before—and Annie nodded her head in time, while the baby positively crowed with delight, and Bessie sat down on the ground, contentedly sucking her thumb, and no one came to them and tried to send them away, as Annie had half feared, so that she soon forgot the feeling of strangeness. Then there was preaching, but what it was about the poor ignorant girl could not make out—only that the "parson," as she called him, was talking about some One Who loved them, and Who would make them good and happy, instead of being sinful and miserable, if they would but go to Him. But when more lights were on the altar, when the cloud of incense went up before God, and the Benediction Service began, Annie almost held her breath ; and seeing that every one else was kneeling—even Dick Turner— she slipped down on her knees too, and never stirred till all was over.

"Didn't I tell you it was splendid!" said Dick triumphantly, as they all went home together more quietly than was usual. "Ain't that something like a church! I shouldn't mind being a Catholic myself, if that's their goings-on."

"You!" said Annie scornfully. "I don't suppose they'd want you, Dick Turner. But what was the parson a-talking about?"

"He ain't a parson—he's a priest. I've found out that's the name of him."

"Well, then, the priest," repeated Annie— "when he was a-preaching, you know, Dick?"

"Oh, I didn't listen," said Dick frankly. "It's the music, and the lights, and the singing I cares for."

"Was it just the same this morning, Dick?"

"No," answered the boy; "it wasn't exactly the same, though I can't tell the difference like. The priest was dressed up in other things, and there wasn't that same kind of singing. He had a lot of it all to himself, and them folks up by the organ did the rest. As for them as was in the seats, round about where we was to-night, Annie, they only seemed to read out of books, and sometimes they'd stand, and then they'd kneel, and two or three times they sat down, and I can't for the life of me think how they knew which to be at, for I didn't hear the priest tell them.   And, Annie, d'ye know, some of 'em had got strings of beads, and wasn't they a-counting of 'em just!   I couldn't make that out, no how."

"Lor, Dick!" exclaimed Annie, who felt those were the strangest doings she ever heard of; but there was no more talk then, for she had come to their own home, and she dragged herself, Bessie, and the baby up—up—up to the very top floor and into a little room, which had only two beds in it, a table, and three chairs, by way of furniture.

No one was there but " Jack," who had not been of the chapel-going party, and a thin, delicate-looking woman, evidently Annie's mother, by the likeness between them.

" Where've you been, Annie?" she said. " Haven't I told you times enough not to go dragging the baby out this time of night?"

"We've only been to the church, mother—the new one, up Leonard Street.   It's beautiful!" said Annie, setting down the baby as she spoke, with a sigh of relief.

" So warm," put in Bessie.

" Well, I'm glad you've been warm for once,"
said the mother. " It's more than I am, sitting
up here without a bit of fire, and this the 8th
of December."

Annie stood a bit, thinking. " Mother, do
you know the priest says there's some One as'd
make all the people in the church good and
happy, if they liked. Did he mean he'd do it
himself ?"

" I'm sure I don't know," said the woman ;
" you'd best have gone and asked him, straight
away."

" Oh, mother ! I couldn't. I shouldn't have
known what to say. But, mother, Dick Turner
says some of the folks there take strings of beads
with 'em. Do you believe it ?"

" Yes, I believe that much," said the mother.
" They're Catholics goes there ; and I remember
a girl I knew, when I was a little thing, and
she was one of that sort, and she had some of
them beads, and she told me she said a prayer
for every one. That's all I know, child."

" Oh !" said Annie, and then began thinking,
feeling more than ever puzzled.

Next day, when Annie was in her usual seat

in the doorway, she saw Dick Turner lounging
by, and she called to him across the street.

"Dick ! here !"

"What d'ye want ?"

"When'll there be more goings-on at that
there place ?"

"You'll hear the bell a-ringing, I s'pose, as
soon as me. *I* don't know."   And Dick was off.

But Annie was not going to be put off that
way.   Once more snatching up the baby, she
took her way to Leonard Street, and to her
great joy the church door was open.   She
peeped in.   Ah ! there were no candles now, no
music, no preaching ; and feeling disappointed,
she was going away, when the little red light
before the altar caught her eye, and she stopped
to gaze at it and wonder what it was burning
there for when it was quite day, and the sunshine streamed in at the windows.   Next she
noticed many things which she had taken no .
heed of the night before — several figures, one
particularly of a lady with a child in her arms,
which Annie thought was beautiful, near which
there were numbers of flowers.   Then she
stepped a little farther inside the church, to
look at some pictures she saw there.   One had

such a kind face that she wondered if the
Person who would make every one good and
happy was like that; and she was gazing at
it so earnestly, that she did not know any
one was near, until she felt a touch on the arm.

It was a lady, who was attracted by the
girl's inquiring face and ragged dress, and now
spoke to her, asking if she liked that picture.

" Yes, ma'am, very much," said Annie, " but
I don't know who it is."

" It is a picture of the Sacred Heart," said
the lady; " it is Our Lord Jesus Christ."

" Oh, I don't know Him," said Annie. " I
thought, maybe, it was him the parson—no, I
mean the priest—was a-talking of last night."

" Were you here last night ?"

Annie nodded. " Yes, me and Dick Turner,
and some more folks from our street. Will
there be anything like it again ?"

" Oh yes," was the answer; " sometimes in
the week, and always on Sunday; and you
can come whenever you like. Do you know
any prayers ?"

Annie shook her head.

" If I taught you one, very short and easy, do
you think you'd remember it ?"

"I'd try," said Annie. "Is it the prayer they say with them beads?"

"No, that is longer; you must learn that after," said the lady, smiling. "This is what I want you to say: 'O God, send Thy Holy Spirit to teach me.'"

Annie repeated it several times quite correctly. "I'll not forget," she said, nodding her head.

"That's right. Say it very often, and you may be quite sure you will learn to be good and happy by-and-by. Now I want you to remember one more thing—will you try?"

Annie smiled.

"You see the red light which burns there before the altar. It is lighted always because Our Lord is there; you cannot see Him, but He is looking at you now. Whenever you come into church, or go out, will you kneel just a moment, to show Our Lord you know He is there?"

Annie promised she would. "And I'll make Dick Turner and my brother Jack do it too," she added.

"Yes, do," answered the lady; "and now, good-bye; I shall look out for you again Don't forget your prayer."

Annie's eyes sparkled with pleasure as she moved towards the church door, then looking at the red light before the altar, knelt as she had been told. She made a funny picture enough in her old ragged frock, which was too short, and a tattered green petticoat, which was as much too long ; but Jesus and Mary loved that dark, sin-stained soul, and the angels in heaven rejoiced because they knew that another child was coming back to God.

"Thy Holy Spirit." Poor Annie Marsh thought of those words over and over again, as she went home that cold December morning. What did they mean? she wondered ; however, she was quite resolved to say the prayer very often, because she felt sure that in some way it was going to make her "good and happy," as the lady had said.

"O God! send Thy Holy Spirit to teach me," she said aloud, as she turned the corner of the last street, running straight against Dick Turner, who was coming the other way.

"I say, Annie Marsh, was you talking to yourself?" he cried.

"That ain't your business," said Annie

sharply, vexed at being overheard. "Look here, Dick Turner; when you go into that Catholic place and come out, you just look at the red lamp and kneel down a minute, will you ?"

"No," said Dick, "I shan't. What's the use of it ?"

"I tell you you must," cried Annie. "I promised the lady for you when she told me—it's because some One's there, Dick, Who sees us quite plain though we don't see Him."

Dick gave a long whistle. "Don't tell me—I ain't a-going to believe any one's there unless I see 'em. What did the lady say ?"

So Annie repeated as well as she could what had been told her, whereupon Dick laughed loudly, to her great annoyance, but she noticed that next time he went in the church to hear the music, he knelt like the rest, in spite of all he had said.

After that, as she dragged the heavy baby about so wearily by day, or lay down on the miserable bed so cold and hungry by night, Annie Marsh was always repeating the words which had been taught her, and Jack joined in too, very often kneeling down in the corner of the room.

" What are you at ?" asked the mother sometimes.

" We're praying for that Holy Spirit," said Jack. " Will it come soon, Annie ?"

" I don't know ; but it'll sure to come by-and-by ; the lady said so."

" Well, I'm sure I don't know what you're after," said their mother. " It's most time you got what you're asking for, I'm thinking. Why don't you ask the priest to tell you when it'll come ?"

" Do you think I might, mother ?" said Annie. " D'ye think he'd mind ?"

" I can't say, child. I suppose he's there to tell folks what they want to know, and he'd tell you the same as the rest."

Many a time after that, when she visited the little church, Annie looked wistfully at the priest, longing to ask him about the Holy Spirit, but she was afraid.

She had not happened to see the lady she had spoken to since the day she had been taught her prayer, but at last, one evening, she caught sight of her, and, forgetting all her shyness, went straight to her, and seizing her hand, exclaimed, "Will it come soon, that I've been praying for ? Oh, I wish some one would teach me.   I want to be happy and good."

"There !   I think the Holy Spirit *has* come to give you that wish," said her friend. "Will you go with me to the priest, and tell him how you want to love God and be good ?"

Annie nodded. "I'll go," she said. "I'd have gone long ago.   Mother said I'd better—but I didn't like."

That night Annie Marsh did not run home in her usual wild way—she even passed her own brother in the street without seeing him—for her head was quite full of what the priest had been telling her. One thing had sunk very deeply into Annie's mind—that some One *loved* her ! *Her*—a poor, dirty, ignorant child, who hardly knew what a kind word was ; and this was "Jesus "—whose picture had attracted her notice in the church.   And she heard now that all day long while she was quarrelling and fighting, and doing so many wrong things, He saw her all the time, and yet He kept on loving her and pitying her so much because she did not know how to be good.

" Don't you think you could learn me how?"
Annie had asked. And the priest had said,
" Oh yes ;" but that she must come to him the
next day, because it was too late then, and he
would try to help her to please God and be one
of His children.

It wasn't much sleep Annie Marsh had that
night. When she got in her mother was very
cross with her for staying out so late, and she
dared not tell her where she had been ; "she
would keep it for another time, when the baby
had been crying and put mother out of temper," she said to herself. However, she
managed to whisper to Jack that she had asked
the priest at the church to teach her how to
be good, and was going to begin to-morrow,
" straight away."

" Mother won't let you go," said Jack.

" Oh yes, she will," answered Annie. " She's
cross to-night, but maybe she'll feel different in
the morning, and she'll let me go, for she's told
me times enough I'd best ask the priest to tell
me how to get that Holy Spirit that's so long
a-coming."

Annie was quite right in her expectation, for
when she asked her mother next day if she

could go to the Catholic church, the answer was, " Yes, you can go where you like, only get out of my way, and take the little ones along with you."

Not many minutes after, a ragged little group stood at the priest's door, waiting for the bell to be answered : Annie with the baby in her arms, and a little child holding her frock on each side ; while Jack stood about a yard off, with his eyes very widely opened, watching to see what would happen next. Even Father Carey could not keep back a smile as he opened the door to them himself, and Annie, dropping a very low curtsey, tugged in vain at the little ones to make them do the same.

" Why, you are the little girl who was to come and see me this morning, aren't you ?" said the priest. " But who are all these ?"

" Mother wouldn't let me come without 'em, sir," said Annie. " I hope you won't mind. Bessie, where's your curtsey, you naughty child ?" But Bessie paid no heed, only stared harder at the kind face which looked down at her, while Jack drew a little nearer the door, and pulled off his cap.

They all went in with the priest to the room

he took them to, and Annie had soon forgotten
any fear she might have felt, and had told him
all about her first going to the Catholic church,
and how she had been praying for the Holy
Spirit ever since " the lady" told her the words.

" And Jack's said it too, sometimes," she
added, giving her brother a little push with her
elbow, which sent him nearer Father Carey,
and brought fresh blushes to the boy's face.

" Well, now you really want to be made
God's children," said the priest, when he had
listened to all they had to say. " Do you know
how that can be done?" Of course they did
not; but they listened as they heard for the
first time that they had souls—a part of them
which could never die, but would live for ever,
either in happiness or misery ; that these souls
were all dark and stained with sin, but that
they could be washed pure and white ; and not
only Annie and Jack, but the little ones, even
the baby, could be made God's own children by
being baptized in the Catholic Church. " Have
you ever heard of baptism?" Father Carey
asked.   But Annie shook her head.   " Have
you never been in other churches and seen
babies christened, as they call it ?" he said,

thinking to make it plainer. But the answer still was No; evidently the little Marshes had not been much acquainted with churches of any kind during their lives. Then the priest explained, as simply as he could, what baptism was, and how it would take away the sin which had been in them ever since they had come into the world as little babies; and Annie begged hard to be baptized then and there.

"Mother wouldn't mind, I'm sure she wouldn't," she added, when Father Carey said he must first speak to their mother, and find out if they had ever been baptized before, and whether she would let them be brought up Catholic children. "Mother'll only say, 'Go where you like, and don't bother me.' She isn't well, you see, sir, and it puts her out to have all the little ones round, and she clears us out whenever it's fine enough. She knew we was a-coming to-day, and she didn't mind a bit."

However, Annie had to be content to wait until the afternoon, when the priest promised to go to their house and speak to their mother; which he did, and found, as Annie had said, that Mrs. Marsh was quite willing that anything should be done with her children which did not give her trouble.

"I don't mind, I'm sure, sir," she said. "I don't suppose it's much difference whether they're Catholics or not. I don't trouble my head about them sort of things ; but I'm sure if you like to christen them, you're welcome. P'r'aps it'll do them good, and any way it can't hurt them."

It was in vain that Father Carey tried to make her understand the need that her children should be baptized ; so, finding it had never been done before, and that she made no objection, it was settled that Annie, Jack, and the little ones should all come to the Catholic church and be made " God's children " next day.

" And then you must give up running about the streets, and come to our schools and learn to be good Catholics," the priest said, as Annie let him out at the door, with a low curtsey and a bright smile, going back to their little dark top room with a happier heart than she had ever known before, to talk over all that had happened that day, and the still more wonderful thing which was to happen to-morrow, with Jack and her mother.

Next morning the poor, ignorant children stood at the font, the bright winter sunshine streaming in upon their earnest wondering faces.

"Now, Annie, you are God's child," said the priest, laying his hand kindly on her head. "Go and kneel down before Jesus, and tell Him how you want Him to help you to keep your soul white."

The child quite understood his meaning. The thought of Jesus always there in the church had filled her mind from the first time she had heard it. She could not have told any one how it was, or why, but it was enough for her to believe that He heard what she said, and would do it, and as she knelt in the church, gazing straight at the red altar-light, with the baby in her arms and the other little ones clustered round her, her whole heart was in her prayer, though the words were so few and simple, as she said—"Dear, kind Jesus, thank you for washing us white, and making us God's children. Please help us all to be good."

A few days after, Annie Marsh was going regularly to the girl's school belonging to the Catholic church, while Jack had his place with the boys, and the little ones were received amongst the babies. It seemed a new, strange life to these children, but they liked it far better than the old times in the street, and tried to learn, because—as Annie said to Jack—"We must get on and understand our religion ready for God to give us His Holy Spirit, Father Carey says."

"Why, I thought we'd got It now?" said Jack.

"Yes, we've got some. We're always getting some, Jack. It's the Holy Spirit made us want to be good ; It makes us wish for everything that's right. But when we have learned a bit more, we'll be 'confirmed,' Father Carey says, and that means God's Holy Spirit will come more than ever. I don't rightly know how to say it, Jack, but I think somehow it is to finish up our being baptized."

"Oh!" said Jack, looking very much puzzled. "Then we'd best keep on that prayer, Annie. I'd left it off myself, but I'll begin again now, till the Holy Spirit comes." And so they did.

Winter had passed by, spring over long ago, and the summer was getting to an end, for the few trees which grew about the town of Clayford lost some of their leaves with every puff of wind or shower of rain which passed over them. Things seemed much the same in that place ; women loitered at the doors of their houses, and ragged children clustered at the street corners, just as they had always done, and yet many besides Jack and Annie Marsh had been gathered into the school of the little Catholic chapel in Leonard street, and many more would drop into the church during its services, and look, and listen, and wonder; some to forget it all next minute, others to laugh and mock, others to think about it, and come again and again. All this while Father Carey had worked on amongst his poor, often weary, often saddened by the sin and misery which came in his way, and yet feeling sure God's work was growing in that ignorant, uncared-for town. The months which had come and gone since the winter day when Annie Marsh with her little brothers and sisters were brought into the Catholic Church had made a great change in the children. They were poor enough still, often hungry, often badly clothed, but they were cleaner, quieter, and happier, and had learned many things which had been all new and strange at first. Their home was still in the little room, at the top of the dirty house in Edward's-street, but it certainly was kept a trifle cleaner, for Annie was growing to feel ashamed of cobwebby windows and unscrubbed floors, and her Saturday's holiday was usually spent in giving the place a " tidying," as she called it. Mrs. Marsh had been quite willing for her children to attend the Catholic schools at first. It took them out of the way for several hours daily, and that was worth a good deal, she thought; and they certainly quarrelled less, and were more dutiful to her, she admitted, since they had been to the church and school so regularly ; but now, after all these months, a change had come over her suddenly, and she told Annie one Friday evening that neither she, Jack, nor the little ones should go to Leonard-street any more.

At first Annie had paid little heed, thinking it was only " mother's temper," which would pass off before Monday came; but when the week began, and she found it was no empty threat, the girl was in the greatest trouble.

" You needn't get them ready, Annie," Mrs.

Marsh had said, as Annie prepared, as usual, to dress the little ones for school; "they ain't a-going any more, nor you either; I've had enough of it."

"But, mother——" began Annie.

"Come, now, don't begin bothering. I've said you shan't go any more, and I'll stick to it; so there."

It came out after a while why the change was. A lady, belonging to the Protestant church near by, had been calling at all the houses in that street; and finding, after a good deal of questioning, that Mrs. Marsh had allowed her children to be baptized Catholics, and to attend the church and schools, she had scolded her angrily, and went with the case to the clergyman, who had himself been to visit the poor woman, and to get her to promise to remove the children at once.

"And he did go on at me, to be sure," said Mrs. Marsh, in telling Annie what had happened. "And when he asked me if your father hadn't lived and died a Protestant, and what I thought he'd have said at you all turning Catholics, I declare it made me come all over in a fright, for I'm sure I never thought it made much difference. However, I promised the parson you shouldn't go any more, and he said there'd be heaps of coal-tickets and soup-tickets give away from his church, and he should think with a large family, and me a widow, I'd be glad of a little help."

" But, mother," said Annie, " I *can't* go to his church, no more can the others. We're Catholics, mother, and we can't give it up for coal-tickets and soup-tickets."

" Come, now, don't you give me any of your ' can'ts and won'ts,' " exclaimed Mrs. Marsh, who was getting angry. " You may call yourself a Catholic if you like, but the whole lot of you'll go to the parson's school this week, or my name's not what it is."

" I *can't* go, mother," Annie said again. " Oh, please let me go and tell the nuns and Father Carey. They'll wonder why we're not at school ; and now, too, when the confirmation's coming so soon. Mother, you'll let me and Jack be confirmed, won't you ? It's God's Holy Spirit coming to make us good Christians, mother—' soldiers of Jesus Christ ;' it's what we've been praying for so long ; and you'll let us go, won't you ?"

" I don't know what you're talking about. Good Christians indeed! Why don't you do as I tell you? you'd be a better girl then than for all this church-going. I'm not a scholar myself, but I've heard tell of the commandments. They've got 'em painted up in the church me and your poor father that's dead and gone were married at. I haven't been in a church since that day—fourteen years come next Whitsuntide—but I dare say they're there now, and I'm pretty sure one of 'em says you're to honour your father and mother. I suppose they don't learn you that at your church."

" Oh yes, mother! it's the fourth commandment, and we're taught that we must obey you in all things that——"

" Come, then," struck in Mrs. Marsh triumphantly, " you go to the parson's school like a good child, and bring along some of them soup-tickets; we'll wan't 'em with winter coming on and things as dear as they are now."

" But, mother, you didn't hear the end of it; it's in ' all things that are not sin,' and it would be sin to give up our own religion for one that's no use, and will only lose us our souls."

" You tell me it's a sin to go where they'll

help your poor mother as works night and day to get bread for you five children, do you ?" screamed the woman, now evidently angry. " If I don't go and tell the parson myself! This is what you've learnt at them precious schools, is it ? I'm sorry enough I ever let you go." A quarter of an hour afterwards, poor Annie found herself with the younger children safely locked in their small room, for her mother had taken the key when she went off to her day's work, saying that she knew if she did not they would " be off to them Catholics " as soon as her back was turned; but she did not notice in her passion that Jack was not there ; he had slipped quietly out while his mother had been talking, and made his way to the priest with all the haste he could.

" Oh, Father !" he had cried breathlessly, " can't you come round to our place ? Mother's a-slipping into Annie like anything, and she says we shan't come to these schools no more."

" But what has happened, then ?" asked Father Carey. " I don't understand it. Your mother was quite willing for you to be Catholics, and you have been regular at school so long. What has changed her so suddenly ? I'm afraid you have been behaving badly, and bringing a disgrace on your faith."

"No, indeed, Father," said Jack earnestly. "It isn't us—it's the parson. He's been round to our place a-blowing up mother for letting us come to this church, and promising her souptickets and things if she'll take us away."

Father Carey looked grieved—not surprised, for such things were familiar enough to him in his rounds of parish work. "Is your mother at home now?" he asked; "I'll go and see her if she is."

"It's her day for going out a-washing," said Jack; "she goes half a day on Mondays to Mrs. Smith's, up James-street; but she hadn't gone when I came here."

"And how was it she let you out, then?" asked Father Carey, putting on his coat, and looking round for his hat.

Jack grinned broadly. "Oh, I hooked it," he explained. "I wasn't a-going to stop there for nothing. I thought I'd best cut round here directly, and tell you what was up."

"Quite right," said the priest; "I dare say I can get your mother to think better of it. Come along, Jack."

But when Jack and Father Carey landed at the top of the dark, steep stairs, they heard the baby crying and Annie singing to it, but no sound of angry voices or disputing; so Jack, whose courage had been oozing away during his ascent of the stairs, grew bold once more and tried to open the door, but in vain. Here was a pretty state of things! The priest and the boy looked at each other in the dusky half-light of the dark staircase, and wondered what it all meant.

"Mrs. Marsh," said Father Carey's pleasant voice, as he tapped at the door with his fingers, "will you let me come in and see you?" But there was no reply; the baby cried louder, and Annie sung on, evidently not hearing the knock or the voice.

"I'd bet anything mother's cleared out and took the key!" exclaimed Jack; then, turning to the door, he put his mouth to the key-hole, and shouted to his sister so vigorously, that even the baby stopped crying from astonishment.

"Is that you, Jack?" said Annie. "We're locked in, and mother's took the key."

"What a bother!" returned Jack; then with

his mouth at the key-hole again, "Here's Father Carey—here along of me; he's come to talk to mother."

"Oh, Father!" cried Annie from the inside, "mother's going to send us all to the Protestant school, and she says she's sorry she ever let us be Catholics; and, oh, Father! can't we be confirmed? Won't you ask mother? for we've been waiting all this time, and—and—" But then Annie could get no further; she just burst out crying, and the little ones followed her example, and made a regular chorus of it. Poor Father Carey! It was hard work to comfort the child, amidst so much noise—through a key-hole, too; but he tried what he could do.

"Annie! leave off crying," he said, "and listen to me. You shall not be sent to the Protestant schools if I can possibly help it, and I think I shall be able to get your mother to feel differently. Try now to trust God to take care of you. Remember nothing can happen to hurt you really if you keep close to Him; so pray with all your heart to our Blessed Lady, and brighter times will come."

Annie wiped her eyes then and felt ever so much better, and, as she listened to Father

Carey's footsteps as he went down the stairs again with Jack behind him, she seemed quite sure that he would find a way to help them out of their trouble.

"And now, Jack, what's to become of you to-day?" said the priest, when he was in the street again.

"Oh, I'm going to the school, same as usual," said the boy. "I can't get in till mother comes home this evening."

So he did; and when he went to the little top room after school was over, he was surprised to find that he was not asked any questions about where he had been. The fact was that Annie had set to work after Father Carey's visit and "tidied-up" so successfully, and had a bit of fire burning, and the kettle on, and all things so comfortable when her mother returned, that Mrs. Marsh's heart was softened, and she was quite good-tempered, and did not even mention the dispute of the morning.

Next day, when it was still very early, Annie got up softly before her mother was awake, and getting out a little crucifix which had been given her at school, she said her usual morning prayers, adding, as she always did, " O God, send down Thy Holy Spirit to teach me." As she said the words her eyes filled with tears, for she remembered how fast the day of Confirmation was drawing on—that day which she had so longed and prayed for. Ah! would God let her be disappointed after all? Would He let her mother keep her from Him and from the Sacraments, which were to give her grace and strength? No; *somehow* Annie felt sure all would come right. She would pray hard, and get the Blessed Virgin and the Saints to pray, too, and she would try and leave the rest to God and Father Carey. So when Mrs. Marsh looked curiously at Annie's face, she was surprised to see how quiet it was. "Well, she didn't make so much bother about her church-going as I expected," was the mother's thought. "I don't suppose I need lock the door to-day."

Monday, Tuesday, and Wednesday in that week were gone. Annie and the little children had remained quietly at home. Master Jack had slipped away to school as usual, for, strangely enough, his mother had taken no heed of his doings. Thursday came—Mrs. Marsh's first day at home — and about the middle of the morning Father Carey came in to see her.

The woman's face showed no welcome, but the priest did not appear to notice it. He took the only chair in the room which was not broken when she offered it to him, and began to speak as pleasantly as if nothing unusual had happened; but Mrs. Marsh was far less easy. She had been very dissatisfied with herself when she gave her promise to the clergyman, but not as she had felt during those three days which Annie had borne so patiently; her silence, her efforts to help her mother, had done more for her than hundreds of words and persuasions, and Mrs. Marsh was half inclined to give in and send her back to the Catholic school without any asking.

However, there was the priest; and he had come to speak about the children, Mrs. Marsh was sure; she must make the best she could of it, at any rate.

"Why is Annie at home?" asked Father Carey at last. "I thought she and the little ones were our most regular scholars, Mrs. Marsh."

"They're not a-coming, sir," said the woman.

"Their father lived a Protestant and died a Protestant, and 'tisn't right the children should be another religion; leastways, the parson says so."

"Oh! you attend the Protestant church yourself, then, do you?" asked the priest.

Mrs. Marsh looked foolish. "No, sir; not exactly. I haven't time for church-going myself. I work too hard in the week. But anyway, I don't hold with the Catholics."

"I am glad you have told me so," said Father Carey; "I like to know what people think about these things. When persons begin to think, it shows that God is knocking at their heart; so many go on without appearing to care about any religion, and that is the worst state of all. Now what is there in the Catholic faith you don't 'hold with,' Mrs. Marsh?"

She was fairly caught then, for she had not a word to say for herself. However, Mrs. Marsh thought she would not give in without a struggle, so she replied she "didn't hold with none of it;" but to the next question of what she "held with" in the Protestant Church she had nothing ready at all.

"I've promised the parson the children will

go to his church, and so they shall!" was the only thing which she could say.

" Well, Mrs. Marsh, I have promised God to try and help these children save their souls, and I mean to keep my word. Now, which do you want them to do when they die—go to heaven or hell ?"

Of course Mrs. Marsh said heaven ; she had never given the subject a thought since the children had been born into the world, and yet, when the question was put, she could not say that she did not care. But when Father Carey spoke plainly to her, telling her that if her children were to go to heaven after death they must prepare for it in this world, and the only way to do so was to belong to Christ's Church and get from that all the grace and help they needed, her carelessness changed to uneasiness, and her uneasiness grew so extreme that she ended by bursting into tears and declaring that, " between one and the other, she was fairly bothered to death."

" But I do not wish to ' bother ' you," said the priest kindly. " I want you to understand why it is of very great consequence to which church you send your children. People say it

' doesn't matter,' and they will find out in the next world it has 'mattered' a great deal. Mrs. Marsh, God has made these little ones His own children ; He is listening now to what you say, and to what I say. Tell me if you mean to keep them away from all the blessings and graces He wants to give them ; tell me if you will run the risk of these children saying to you, in years to come, that you have made them lose their souls ?"

" No, no !" said Mrs. Marsh, wiping her eyes with her apron. " I didn't think of all that, I only promised the parson ; but they shall keep to the Catholics, sir, after what you've said, and I must say they've been a deal better children since they took to coming. Yes, sir, they shall all come to-morrow morning, you may be sure."   And with a glad heart she saw her visitor down the stairs, for she had never before felt quite so uncomfortable.

" Lor ! how them priests do come over a body," she exclaimed, as she returned to her room once more. " I never meant to let him get the best of it, but he did, after all ! Well, there'll be no soup and no coals from the parson after this."   And Mrs. Marsh was cross all the evening in consequence, and pushed the children here and there, and scolded Annie, and boxed Jack's ears into the bargain; but they did not much care—they were so glad that "mother had said they should go back to school next day."

"Dress the children, and take yourselves off to your precious schools, and don't let me hear anything about it!" was the order next morning; and Annie obeyed with the greatest haste, and went back to the nuns with the lightest of hearts after her four days' imprisonment.

That was the last time that the little Marshes heard anything about the Protestant schools. How their mother settled it with the parson she never told them; they only knew that for a little while she was very cross and harsh, and then fell back again into her old habit of indolence and carelessness, scolding now and then, but usually letting them take their own way.

It was the custom of leaving the children to care for themselves which had made Annie and Jack spend the first part of their lives almost entirely in the streets; it was this which would have been their ruin if God had not drawn them within the safety of His Church, where they learned the danger of temptation, and received the needful grace to resist it when it came. That had been, indeed, a happy day for the neglected children when they first heard the bell of the little mission chapel in Leonard-street—first stood in the presence of their God and Saviour, Whose very nearness made itself felt in those darkened hearts while yet they were unconscious of it.   But another day was drawing on—a happy day, too—so long desired, so prayed for.

The little town was all in a stir and bustle ; Leonard-street was crowded with men, women, boys, girls, and babies of all ages and descriptions ; for there was to be a Confirmation at the Catholic church, and the Bishop was coming, and all Clayford had turned out to see him.

Inside, the little building was full of children with softened, earnest faces, and half-glad, half-timid hearts, waiting for the Sacrament which was to strengthen the faith which had been given them at their Baptism, to put them in the ranks of Christ's soldiers, with many a hard battle before them to fight against sin, against self, against the world ; but such an immense strength to fit them for it by the coming of the Holy Ghost upon them.

No one there was thinking more seriously of what she was about to do than Annie Marsh. Many an one was of a higher station, many an one had been trained and taught from infancy to expect and desire this sacrament of Confirmation, but yet all had not Annie's longing to receive it. Though she was but a child, she knew better than many of her age what temptations were all around her, and she knew, too, that by herself she was too weak to keep good, but that with the power of God's Holy Spirit she should be safe. As she knelt there in her neat blue frock and white veil, her thoughts travelled back to the day she had first been taught to ask God for this beautiful gift; it was hers now, and her heart throbbed with joy, not fear, as she went back to her place with her eyes quite full of happy, grateful tears.

Ah! how she thanked God that day for herself and for Jack—little Jack, whose face shone again with the scrubbing she had given it, and whose clothes had been brushed up to look as nice as possible. I don't know that she said many words, but her heart told the feelings she could not have spoken, and that was what Jesus looked at and loved,

Mrs. Marsh was in the church, looking at her children with some pride, some feelings of pain: the pride was to see them so neat, so clean, so happy-looking; the pain because she knew they had got something which was not hers, that the peace on their faces came from One of Whom she knew nothing; and there, in the quiet corner, the mother felt her first desire for a better and different life to that which she had hitherto led. If Annie had only known this, another joy would have entered her heart; but she *did* know her mother was there, and that gave her great happiness, for she believed that her first visit to the little church would not be the last. God had heard and answered her first prayer — she would begin to say another every night and morning, and that should be for "mother," that she also might come into Christ's true Church, and get this Holy Spirit, with its seven gifts of grace, and the beautiful fruits which come from it, and thus escape the misery of offending God in this world and being separated from Him for all eternity.

Pat's Rosary, and what came of it.

IN one of the great hospitals of London, a little boy of some nine years or more, sat by the window of the ward with a weary look on his small thin face —a look of sorrow more than of pain, for Pat Magrath was better, and in another week would be discharged quite recovered of the injuries which had brought him there.

He was thinking of home that bright spring afternoon—his wretched home and rough, bad mother. Oh, how different it would be from the orderly hospital and the quiet, gentle nurses who had been so kind to him—all the pain and helplessness seemed worth bearing for the sake of the comfort which was a new experience in his poor miserable little life.

Pat met with his accident one Saturday
night — that time of all others when from
the back streets and alleys of London there
rises a tumult which is very terrible to the
more decent poor compelled by misfortune
to live in such surroundings, where coarse
shouts and oaths mingle with the sound of
blows and other personal violence.

In Golden-court that night, Pat's own
mother was engaged with another woman in
settling a quarrel after the ordinary manner.
Bill Green had broken one of the panes of
Bridget Magrath's window, and the fiery-
tempered Irishwoman was going to "tache
him betther" by attacking the one who sup-
ported him in all his wrong-doings.

A mob had gathered round the combatants.
From the adjoining houses, men, women, and
children poured, jostling and pushing each
other to witness the battle and shout encouragement to which of the two they felt most
disposed to favour.

Pat was not unused to see his mother fight,
but he generally fared worse afterwards, when
she had refreshed herself at the nearest gin-
palace, so that his custom was to get out of

the way for the night, as he did upon this occasion.

How it happened that he—so well accustomed to dodge between cabs and carriages, or dive under the heads of horses—should be knocked down by a hansom cab, Pat could never understand. However, so it was, and all bleeding and unconscious from the cuts about his head, and with one arm broken and hanging limply at his side, he was conveyed to the hospital, where he roused up to find himself in the surgeon's hands.

So, as we have said, the days and weeks had passed by, and the little Irish boy was nearly well, and nearly ready too for being sent back to the wretched home in one of the houses of Golden-court.

Pat was thinking sorrowfully of going to his mother again, but he was wondering, too, how he could possibly succeed in doing something he very much wished and had been praying for every day. To tell you what this desire was, to tell you too how Pat had learned to pray at all, I must go back to a day when at the very worst of his pain and weariness a kind face had bent over him, and a voice, which seemed the sweetest he had ever heard, asked his name.

"Patrick Magrath," was the answer; and then the lady sat down by the bed and talked gently to the little boy, telling him that as he was Irish he must surely be a Catholic, and if a Catholic one of those whom she came there especially to see.

It was very pleasant to feel that he had some-one to see him at last. On certain days people came to visit those who lay ill in the hospitals: wives to sit awhile with their husbands, mothers to see their children, and yet no one ever for Pat Magrath, except once when his mother came, bringing in such a smell of spirits and talking so loudly that he could only be very glad when she had gone away, and hope she would come no more—which hope was fulfilled.

But here was a visitor—a kind, sweet-voiced lady who looked at Pat as if she had always known and cared about him—a lady so nicely dressed, that the other inmates in the ward watched her as she passed with evident admi-ration—such admiration as the poor feel natu-rally for what is tasteful and pleasant to the eye.

She asked him few questions, but they were enough to enable her to make sure that he was wholly untaught in the faith of his baptism, even before Pat told her what sort of life he had led—how his mother never went to church but on Good Friday and Christmas Day, and never stayed long enough in any one place for a priest to find out her and her boy.

But this was, as I have said, at the early beginning of Pat's hospital life, and since then great things had been done. I could never tell you how patiently this kind visitor had sat day by day at the little boy's side, teaching him of Jesus and Mary; I could never tell you how often she had repeated the Church's prayer to that Blessed Mother, until it had become imprinted on the dulled mind, and Pat could say it for himself, understanding all he meant by it. A priest had come to the little suffering boy, brought there by the same kind friend, and then Pat had told out the many sins of his brief life, and received the pardon of Jesus the Son of Mary; nay, more than this, for on one day when no one felt very sure of the child's recovery, when fever had parched his lips and wasted his small strength, the Blessed Sacrament of love had been brought into that sick ward, and Pat knew that it was Jesus, Whose word and touch healed soul and sometimes body too, now, as in the olden time when He dwelt on earth. Great things, were they not ? You will not wonder now that Pat Magrath's hospital life seemed an era he could never, never forget.

So now that he was going so soon back to the rough bad world in which he dwelt, Pat's friends had bidden him pray earnestly for himself, and pray too for his mother, that she might turn from the evil of her life.

He had a rosary, his chief, and indeed his only treasure, and upon this rosary he said daily the prayer which he had learned quite perfectly, offering it for his mother—the sin-stained godless woman who had perhaps never since her childhood prayed for herself.

"It seems most too good to be true that mother should get better," said the boy to the priest; but Father Farley had bidden him keep on praying daily with a strong faith in Mary, who loves to obtain the mercy of her Son for sinners.

Very sorrowfully when the day came did Pat take leave of the hospital; another boy from his ward was going out too, but. *his* mother came to meet him, and seemed glad. Pat had no mother to clasp him in her arms; crying and laughing together in the joy of her heart. Mrs. Magrath might have been found in a certain spirit-vault, clasping a gin bottle as *her* greatest comfort, which she had found money to buy, and take back to the room to which her little boy was making his way sorrowfully and alone.

"Oh, here *you* are," she said when she went in and found Pat standing gloomily by the small, dark window. "Now I hope you're going to begin to get your own living after all this nursing and fussing of you."

Pat did not miss any welcome, for he had never expected it; he felt indeed relieved to see that his mother was unusually sober, and handed him some fragments, which poor folks call "broken victuals," collected from some house where at intervals Mrs. Magrath was supposed to work.

However, if she was partly sober then, it was a state of things which did not continue long under the influence of the black bottle on the mantel-shelf, and when night set in Pat was lying alone and frightened as of old, while his mother was quarrelling with another lodger below ; their voices rising louder and louder until it seemed that harder things than words would certainly follow.

This was the mother for whom he was to pray ! to poor little Pat, any change in her seemed so impossible, so hopeless, that I doubt if he would have kept to his daily rosary only from the promise he had given to his first kind friend, and to Father Farley.

Instructed now in what was his duty, the boy went off to Mass when Sunday came, without any opposition from his mother. Little she cared where he went or what he did with himself, if only he was in the way when she wanted him, and out of the way when she preferred his absence. Once he did venture to ask if she would not come to Mass too, but his only answer was the command to " be off about his business and not meddle with his mother's doin's."

It was very hard for a child like Pat Magrath to keep to church and school without any help or encouragement at home—so hard, that we cannot marvel if now and then he slipped and fell away from right, borne down by strong temptation. But though this happened, there followed always both sorrow and resolve—sorrow for the sin, resolve to confess it, and begin again—so that Pat did not wholly wander from the better path in which he had taken the first steps during his stay at the London hospital.

A year went by, much as previous years had passed, with the exception of the change in the little Irish boy's own way of living—the poverty, the want, the scoldings, revilings, and blows of his drinking mother were just the same, and yet every day the rosary had been said for her.

"It's no use—it's not a bit of use," Pat sobbed to himself many and many a time when he had suffered from her violence; but still he had promised to say the prayer, and something always kept him from giving it up, even when he felt most heartless, and most hopeless concerning the "use" of it.

So once again it was May—just such a soft, warm afternoon as that on which he had come out of hospital a year before. When school was over, and Pat came slowly back to Golden Court, he was thinking of the day when he had said good-bye to all that peace and comfort, of the wretched look of the attic when he came in, even though some sunbeams had found their way there through all the dirt and cobwebs. Yes, it was a year ago, and his mother was as bad, as drunken, as rough-spoken as ever—what use was the rosary he had said so long? That thought seemed to fill Pat's mind; he had never perhaps felt quite so ready to give up all striving to be good, quite so ready to go the way of the other boys of the court, who laughed at the "Roman," as they called him.

Thus thinking, Pat Magrath turned away from his home, even when his foot was on the threshold—he would run about the streets, do something, anything by which to get food, and never see his mother again, *never!*

On and on he went, scarcely looking up, scarcely heeding any one he met, so wrapt was he in the thought of his misery. Suddenly a carriage came clattering up just by where he stood; the horses were reined in, the door opened, and Pat being forced to wait, looked up to see—well, a kind face and those bright soft eyes he had first known in the hospital twelve months before.

He forgot that she was rich, he poor; that she was the well-dressed lady of rank, and he a ragged Irish urchin. Yes, he forgot all this as he ran forward and pulled her by the dress, but then I am glad to tell you that this friend of his forgot it too.

"Do you want anything from me, my little boy?" said the gentle voice.

"Oh, please mum, yes. I'm Pat Magrath— him as you came a-visitin' over at the 'orspital, and taught the rosary. I wants to tell you, mum, as mother isn't no better—I 'most think she's worse, if sich a thing can be and all the prayers I've said are no use."

She knew him then, did this good friend of Pat's, and patiently as ever she listened to his story, with her hand resting on the rough mop of a head.

"Poor little Pat, I have not forgotten you. I will come and see you at home, and see what I can do for your mother;" and then the address, No. 7, Golden-court, was written down in a little note-book at which the Irish boy gazed admiringly. "And now I am going into this church, to pray to Our Lady, for it is her month you know, and we must try and visit her image every day. I will say a rosary there for you and for your mother, and to-morrow I will come."

And with a kind smile she was gone, while Pat remained standing in the street as if he scarcely knew what had been happening. All thought of leaving his mother was gone now; all thought of giving up good and turning to evil ways had vanished from his mind, and the next minute Pat went up the church steps and in through the door by which the lady had entered, resolving that he too would say a special prayer to Mary upon that bright May day.

As the little boy went home, the prospect of what was to happen on the morrow so filled his mind that he forgot all his troubles; nor did he heed the noises of the byways through which he passed, or the shouts of the boys of the court, but trudged up the narrow stairs as one in a happy dream.

Strange to say his mother was there, cowering over a bit of fire, and crying bitterly as she rocked herself to and fro.

" Why, mother," said Pat, " what ails you ?" for such a sight had never met his eyes before.

It took some time for the story to come out, but at last Pat heard that the priest had found Bridget Magrath, after many an effort, and had so spoken to her of the sin and misery of her life that conscience was awakened, and she was crying to think of all the wrong of so many years.

" It's my rosary that's brought him here," said Pat, and then he told his mother the story of his promise, and how he had kept it, though so often tempted to think it a useless task.

You can guess the end of my story, I am sure, so that I need scarcely tell you of how the visit of Pat's dear friend encouraged Bridget Magrath in her resolve to begin a new life, and of how she kept to this resolve, and once restored to God's grace bade farewell to her old companions in Golden-court for ever.

They are as decent and respectable a poor mother and son now as you could wish to see, and if you asked the secret of the change you would be sure to get the story of Pat's rosary, and all the blessings it brought about.

And as the prayer of this little boy was heard and answered, so too will it be with us if we call Mary to our aid. The waiting may, indeed, seem long, but never will it be in vain, for the gentle Mother pleading with her Divine Son will obtain for us all grace and blessing "now, and in the hour of our death."

"Only a Picture."

IT was evening, and Minnie Vernon's sunny little face was pressed against the window, watching for her father's return. The rain fell fast, the great drops plashed on the pavement and pattered against the glass, the foot-passengers hurried by and carriages rolled rapidly along the streets, but the figure for which Minnie watched did not come.

Then the lamplighter passed down the street, and the servant wanted to close the shutters, but Minnie begged her not.

"He *can't* be long, Sarah," she said, turning to the window and peering out into the fast-gathering darkness.

Presently the little girl heard singing; who could be singing in the street on such a night?

Looking closely, Minnie saw two figures, a woman and child, who stood opposite the house singing an old song which they hoped would attract the notice of some kind-hearted person and win them a few pence.

"Oh, poor things, how cold and wet they must be! Sarah, do please come with me to the door, and I'll give them a penny," said the little girl, and Sarah agreed.

A very miserable ragged child came up the steps when the door opened, and began a whining tale, part true and part false, of how 'father was dead, and mother couldn't get any work, and five little brothers and sisters at home crying for food."

Minnie Vernon loved poor people, for were they not God's poor? and the thought of the little ones crying for food would have drawn all the money from her own small purse, but then she had not much in it—only two-pence.

"Papa hasn't come home, and I have only got this," she said, putting the two coins in the dirty hand outstretched to receive them. "I wish I had more to give you; but do you like pictures ?"

"Yes, miss," said the little beggar, and Minnie ran to the dining-room, opened a drawer which held some of her own special property, and returned with one of the small sacred pictures in her hand which Catholic children love.

"See how pretty this is," she said. "This little child is the Lord Jesus Christ when He was a baby in this world. See, He stretches out His arms and says 'Come unto me.' You would like it, would you not ?"

"Yes, miss, thank you," said the beggar child, dropping a curtsey ; but when she joined her mother and was asked what she had got, she said, "Only a picture," and kept the pence as a little hidden store for herself.

"A picture !" cried the woman scornfully ; "what's the use of a picture to folks that are starving ? A picture won't give you your supper. Are you telling me a lie now ?" she added, seizing the child roughly by the shoulder. "Didn't she give you so much as a halfpenny ?"

"No, mother, not a farthing," was the answer for Martha Blake had no love of truth in her, and did not scruple to give this reply ; but she grasped the pence tightly under her old bit of a shawl, and laughed to herself as her mother uttered a terrible oath concerning these " rich folks who didn't care who might be starving so long as they had all they wanted."

Singing evidently was useless that wet night, so Mrs. Blake turned in the direction of home, though when she reached the corner of the street she bade Martha "go on," and herself entered a flaunting gin-palace, there to expend the few halfpence she had in her pocket, which ought to have bought bread for the little ones who were waiting in the damp kitchen.

There were not five, as Martha had said in her tale; only two dirty squalid-looking objects, who, worn out with crying, had dropped asleep at last on an old shawl in the corner by the window, which seemed to represent a bed for the family.

Martha was rather glad that Johnnie and " Liz " were sleeping. She was a bad child, yet some feeling still lived in her heart, which made her find it hard to resist them if they asked for food and she had it—now she could slip out to the kidney-pie shop round the corner and spend her twopence and enjoy her supper without any one being the wiser, for " mother " certainly would not be coming home till the hour when the doors of the gin-palace closed upon her.

It was soon done, and Martha having made short work of the savoury morsel, was wishing for more, when a girl came wearily in and sat down upon their one rickety chair with a deep, long-drawn sigh.

" Is she drinking again ?" said this new-comer, glancing at Martha.

The child nodded, and then told of her supper and how she had obtained it, feeling quite sure that her friend would laugh and think it a very clever thing to have accomplished.

"The little lady did give me a picture though," she added; "just as if the likes of me would care for pictures. Here it is too ;" and she pulled from her pocket Minnie Vernon's little print, somewhat crumpled certainly, but not otherwise damaged.

The elder girl laughed, and held out her hand, but when she saw what it was, she flung it down and rose to her feet with a look which Martha had never before seen on her face.

"I'm going out again," she exclaimed, and was off before there was time for any questioning; off into the wet streets, off into the drenching rain and the cold night wind, *anywhere*, if she could forget that little innocent pictured face of Jesus the Son of God.

Kate Brien was no relation of the Blakes; she only lodged there, and no one knew or cared to ask about her friends or her former life, neither did she care to tell of them.

Her story was full of sorrow and of sin. The innocence and purity of childhood had been over while yet she was but a little child, and now that Kate was almost a woman she was familiar with vices and crimes of which we may not speak.

But there had been a time when things were very different; the time when in school and in church she had learned the lessons of her faith, and had received the grace of the sacraments, which had now been forsaken and despised.

Did Kate ever think of those days? well, not often. At first she did; in the first wilful leaving of home and parents she had felt uneasy, and now and then almost resolved to turn back from evil; but she had not done this, and thus each year had seen her become more sinful, more miserable, more hopeless.

Only a picture; but it was one which Kate Brien had seen before in happier days. The very same picture which the priest had given her when she was in the class of children preparing for First Communion, and as her eyes rested on it, she almost seemed to see again the place and the faces of her companions, and to hear once more the earnest, gentle voice of Father Harrison, telling them of Christ Who was saying to each young heart, " Come unto Me ;" of Christ Who waited for each one, Who longed to give Himself to each one, Who would never, never leave their hearts again after that happy First Communion, unless driven from them by grievous sin.

Angrily she dashed along the streets, she felt as if she hated the picture which had roused such recollections, and hated Martha Blake for bringing it home. Yet in spite of this angry, exasperated feeling, there was a longing—oh, how deep, how strong, no words of mine could ever tell you—for the old days when as a child she was getting ready for the visit of Jesus, getting ready for the day when she was to go to Him, to receive Him Who said, "Come unto Me."

"It is all over, nothing can save me," and Kate went on her way little heeding where it led her. Was it by chance that she passed a lighted church, by chance that the sound of music made her first linger and then go in? Oh no; it was all the way of the Good Shepherd, Who was seeking to save His lost sheep.

Why they were singing about that! the dear simple hymn we all know, and which Kate Brien had sung many a time in the school and church near her childhood's home.

> "I was wandering and weary
> When my Saviour came unto me."

Yes—He had come to her that night by means of just a little picture, and Kate could not turn away any more.

Need I tell you the end of her story, of how, in the sweet presence of Jesus, the long-hardened heart became full of sorrow and of love, a sorrow and a love which led her to the feet of Him Whom she had pained with her sins, to lay all the burden there and rise at peace and forgiven?

When the poor girl went back to her lodging, little Martha was asleep as well as the younger children, for the hour was late; but the despised, crumpled picture lay unheeded on the floor till Kate picked it up and, kissing it, put it in a place of safety.

"Come unto Me;" when sin tempted her, when evil companions all but persuaded her, when it seemed so hard, so impossible, to be good, so easy and so pleasant to do wrong, those words were her greatest help.

"Come unto Me;" ah, He did not now pass about the streets and busy thoroughfares of London as once He had walked around and about the towns and villages near Jerusalem, not now did He stand in human presence by the side of the sinful, the sick, and the sorrowing, and yet none the less did He say to her and to all men, " Come unto Me."

Kate had been taught in childhood the blessed lessons of her faith; she knew that it was to Christ in the Blessed Sacrament she must come in the hour of temptation, to kneel there and to pray, to receive Him into her heart with contrite love.

Oh blessed little picture which taught afresh

those lessons too long forgotten! oh happy day when Minnie Vernon gave it into the hand of the street-singer!

It was hard to get out of all the sin and of all the occasions of it, but Kate Brien was not left unaided, for God raises up friends and helpers for those who strive to do right.

You would never think if you saw her now that there was any dark, sad story connected with her past life. So neat, so pleasant-looking, so happy is she, that I would like to show her to you as she goes about her daily work in the household where she has been servant for some years ; you would hardly believe she had ever been the miserable, slatternly, unhappy girl who once shared the Blakes' kitchen.

And what of them ? Kate could tell you how she tried to get the miserable mother out of her sin, tried to persuade the children to learn her faith and love her church ; but tried in vain, until at last they disappeared from her sight into some other miserable haunt of vice and wretchedness, like the many thousands who live by night and by day in the cold homeless streets or forlorn homes and will not be comforted or helped by the loving

Saviour Who dwells in their midst to bless them.

Kate Brien has neat prayer-books now, and many pictures which have been given her by good friends, but I think there is not one she prizes as that which is old, worn, and crumpled, but which was the message of God to her poor sinful, restless, aching heart, which reminded her of One Who never turns from the very vilest and lowest of His creatures when they come to His feet for pardon, and Who will ever say to them, " Thy sins are forgiven thee, go in peace,"

THE END.

R. WASHBOURNE, PRINTER, 18 PATERNOSTER ROW, LONDON.

By M. F. S.

Price 1s. each, cloth, or 1s. 6d. gilt.

1. TOM'S CRUCIFIX, AND PAT'S ROSARY.

2. THE OLD PRAYER-BOOK, AND CHARLIE PEARSON'S MEDAL.

3. GOOD FOR EVIL, AND JOE RYAN'S REPENTANCE.

4. CATHERINE'S PROMISE, AND NORAH'S TEMPTATION.

5. ANNIE'S FIRST PRAYER, AND ONLY A PICTURE.

LONDON :
R. WASHBOURNE, 18 PATERNOSTER ROW.